Praise for

A GOOD HAPPY GIRL

"Redefine quiet quitting with Marissa Higgins's taut debut novel, *A Good Happy Girl*, in which a young lesbian lawyer with a Mariana Trench–size streak of masochism whiles away her work hours posting online videos of her feet in the office restroom, and relitigating the hurts of her Dickensian childhood via sex and self-destruction."

—LEAH GREENBLATT, *The New York Times*

"A sad, sexy ode to the complexity of human connection."

—EMMA SPECTER, *Vogue*

"This is a work of textures, of excess, of grease, of desire. It is a portrait of pleasure as punishment and punishment as pleasure, a gluttonous urge for more until both small joys and small discomforts are compounded into the same nauseating grotesquerie."

—DREW BURNETT GREGORY, *Autostraddle*

"It's impossible to look away or not keep turning the page. Higgins, as the novel demonstrates, is enormously skilled at provoking the reader's empathy for complex, unsavory characters."

—SAMANTHA PAIGE ROSEN, *Interview*

"Marissa Higgins has an addictive and uncanny ability to write about devastating topics with a shrug. It's a talent that's on display in her original and stylish debut novel."

—SOPHIA JUNE, *Nylon*

T0370088

"Higgins masterfully oscillates between poignancy and the grotesque as she examines the many dimensions of both care and neglect." —ELIZABETH ENDICOTT, *Chicago Review of Books*

"Fearless and often shockingly intimate . . . *A Good Happy Girl* enters a reader like ice in the veins." —SAM FRANZINI, *Our Culture Mag*

"A portrait of a person looking for deep connection with others while relentlessly holding herself away from that very thing. Helen's voice springs fully off the page. In gripping (hardcore, fully-embodied) detail, she documents how a small gesture or turn of phrase can unsettle the self and plunge her into the depths of her mind." —MICHAEL COLBERT, *Full Stop*

"Come for the sapphic throuple, but stay for the profound character study, the questions the novel asks without being moralistic, and the razor-sharp sentences . . . This novel does so much and nails it all." —RACHEL LEÓN, *Split Lip Magazine*

"Helen's voice is entirely singular, and you'll keep reading not only because of the impeccable sentences—each one carrying so much weight—but also to find out how deep into desperation Helen will let herself slip before asking to be saved." —KIM NARBY, *Write or Die Magazine*

"If you're a fan of Melissa Broder or Sally Rooney, and have ever wished their work was gayer . . . look no further! . . . A poignant, captivating, observant, and very queer narration following a fraught period of early adulthood."

—TIERNAN BERTRAND-ESSINGTON, *Queerty*

"One of the sexiest, most sensual and sapphic books in recent memory." —ADAM VITCAVAGE, *Debutiful*

"[A] striking and visceral debut . . . Higgins expertly captures the longing and self-loathing that drive Helen's masochism . . . The results are as captivating as they are disturbing."

—*Publishers Weekly* (starred review)

"Sometimes I could not believe how easily this book moved from gross-out sadism into genuine sympathy. Totally surprising, totally compelling. I loved it."

—HALLE BUTLER, author of *The New Me*

"An intensely queer and disarming story about unconventional love. Marissa Higgins's debut is superbly sad, sapphic, and sexy." —EMILY AUSTIN, author of *Everyone in This Room Will Someday Be Dead*

"Combining the bleak New England edge of Ottessa Moshfegh's *Eileen* with the sapphic psychodrama of Yorgos Lanthimos's *The Favourite*, Marissa Higgins's *A Good Happy Girl* is fearless, twisted, and shockingly tender. A fantastic and moving debut."

—ANNA DORN, author of *Exalted*

"Weirdly sexy, propulsive, and darkly funny, *A Good Happy Girl* explores survivor guilt, estrangement, and the thorny roads we take to sabotage, punish, and patch up ourselves. Like a sticky, home-brewed elixir that just might cure you if it doesn't take you down first, Marissa Higgins's debut is hypnotic and deliciously addictive."

—DEB ROGERS, author of *Florida Woman*

"In *A Good Happy Girl*, Marissa Higgins writes beautifully about the painful responsibilities that warp our relationships. This novel is equal parts erotic and grotesque and humane. Higgins writes gracefully about queerness and contradiction, bringing tenderness to the regrets that shape a young life."

—ISLE MCELROY, author of *People Collide*

"*A Good Happy Girl* offers an unwavering look at a young woman for whom wavering has been a way of life. Higgins's heroine makes for a compellingly prickly protagonist, an uncertain someone who the reader nonetheless wants so much to hug. This keen-edged gem of a novel limns the sometimes erotic, often quixotic quest to transcend oneself while trying to retain one's own personhood."

—MICHELLE HART, author of
We Do What We Do in the Dark

"*A Good Happy Girl* is at once a darkly erotic tale, a portrait of a woman on the brink, and a searching exploration of intergenerational poverty and abuse. This is a taut, thorny, and utterly thrilling debut." —ANTONIA ANGRESS,
author of *Sirens & Muses*

A GOOD
HAPPY GIRL

A GOOD

HAPPY GIRL

A NOVEL

Marissa Higgins

CATAPULT   NEW YORK

A Good Happy Girl

Copyright © 2024 by Marissa Higgins

First Catapult edition: 2024
First paperback edition: 2025

Hardcover ISBN: 978-1-64622-197-4
Paperback ISBN: 978-1-64622-267-4

Library of Congress Control Number: 2023943110

Cover design by Sarah Brody
Cover photograph © Stocksy / Luciano Spinelli
Book design by Laura Berry
Elderberry illustrations © Adobe Stock / lovelylittlr

Catapult
New York, NY
books.catapult.co

Printed in the United States of America

1 3 5 7 9 10 8 6 4 2

For we who seek forgiveness

"Animals"

—FRANK O'HARA

A GOOD
HAPPY GIRL

1

I RAN CHARACTERISTICALLY LATE TO meet Catherine and Katrina, and so I took a cab, though I hated sharing confined spaces with men; those were the days before you could request a woman driver. The cab ride did not take long, as I had suggested a cafe only a mile from where I lived. During our introductory phone call—a formality to make sure none of us was a scammer—I told the women about my narrow one-bedroom apartment and its excellent, natural light. It's small, I'd said, turning myself in a circle, naked with bloated belly out and pretty, surveying the space as though to measure my own honesty and accuracy, less to be certain I was not misleading these women whose lives I might change and more to confirm for myself that reality was as I described it. My place isn't much, I continued, but if you two ever wake up here, it gets the warmest light. Oh, Catherine had replied, we certainly plan to check it out. And I felt in her silence that Katrina agreed.

We planned to meet for nonalcoholic drinks at a twenty-four-hour diner to start, a boundary I established as a means of reassuring myself I was not entirely careless with my life. I was unsettled in the months following my parents' incarceration. I had no sibling then and hardly a friend I hadn't hurt. I turned to the apps for sex with greater frequency, telling women who pressed for more that I was having a hard time and could not commit, careful to remind them they were radiant, full of life, and that my opaque behavior was not their fault. The women who did not press gave me a sense of both relief and betrayal. The day I actually met Catherine and Katrina, I did some of what I had done on the day I canceled as well: I scrubbed grime from my blinds with a toothbrush. I hustled to the pharmacy and bought disinfectant wipes for the counter and the toilet rim. I loaded up on decongestants to save my mind. I brushed my teeth, which, in bad spells, I only did a few nights a week. I believed worthy women would detect the mire under my skin. My grime, a game I played with myself: Which women would I clean up for?

I canceled our first date too close to the meeting time—they called me after I texted. We have our scarves on, Catherine said, and though they'd only sent me photos of them in the summer, bikinis at both Revere and Race Point, I envisioned them in plaid scarves without problem. I managed to say I was sorry, so sorry, but offered no real excuse. The time got away from me, I said, thinking of the toothbrushes now coated in months' worth of grime. Catherine tsked me and I thought I would be happy to hear that disappointment frequently.

So when I ran late, again, on the day we rescheduled, I hustled. Snow had fallen overnight and I wondered if I might shatter a bone or two and how I might use their guilt in my favor. As the cab U-turned to pick me up, I snapped a photo of myself and sent it to Catherine and Katrina. I only had one phone number for them at that point: Catherine's. The light was not nearly as good outside, all streetlights and high beams, and the dark circles under my eyes revealed my instability. *Perfect*, they replied. *We're on our way too.* They did not send a picture but I trusted.

Moments later, they added, *We'll probably beat you. If we do, look for us outside.* I put my phone in my pocket and zipped it. I wore a decidedly hideous coat that winter, one I had found at the local thrift shop. A mecca for hipsters as well as the actually poor in the Boston area where the clothes sat in a disorganized heap on the floor and customers weighed them at the checkout register. This very thick coat, which I tried on over the sweater and leggings I'd worn that fall afternoon, came to just under five dollars. In the car, I tugged at the zipper, up down up, and I thought of their names as one word, *CatherineKatrina*, then sounds, *CKCKCKCKCKCK.* My therapist might have called me manic, but she offered compassion-focused therapy for people she described as trauma survivors, so she didn't provide me with the stability of such a label.

When I arrived at the cafe, hands and face red, it was evening, close to six, our scheduled meeting time. I scanned the outdoor seating for my mother, and then my father, and then my dead brother, though I knew none of them were there among the tables. Everything appeared as expected, including Catherine and Katrina sitting not twenty feet from me. There was an empty chair beside them and I hoped they'd had to drag it over themselves. Their photos understated their beauty, and I figured that was a premeditated decision; if they looked too especially lovely, a once-in-a-year kind of beauty, expectations might be too high. But if they looked extraordinarily ordinary in the self-selected photos, in real life, they would garner a level of frisson, even relief. Or perhaps that was only my own rationale in sending out my face, breasts, pubic hair, and feet. My porous understanding of the self was prone to bleeding out. I have never asked them to clarify those early choices.

I walked by the wives and approached the glass door, hoping one or both of them would follow and slam me to the ground. In my daydream, I fell forward mouth open teeth out lips turned up defenseless—I never smiled when I could help it in those days but my fantasy self was finally getting what I wanted, the quick satisfaction of being chased and captured. My dream self slurped vaginal fluid from the pavement no oil no grime no dust only the good stuff and thanked the wives for soothing me with their sharp laughter. In my lived life I didn't even turn my head.

Understand even then I wanted to be equal parts desired and far-flung.

2

A HOSTESS AND WAITRESS LOOKED AT the same piece of laminated paper and frowned. I wanted to stand between them and help sort it out: Had she been assigned one too many tables before her shift ended? Or the opposite, had she been shafted and now look, her tips weren't quite what she expected, and was that really fair? I wanted to kiss them both on the mouth.

From behind me, I heard Catherine say, Helen? She did not clear her throat nor reach out and touch my shoulder or my back. In person, her voice suggested better potential for yelling; she possessed the sort of vocal fry that made men change radio stations and comforted women like myself. I wanted to step farther from her, force her to speak louder and louder. But I was afraid of her then, unsure she'd know how to play my games, and so I turned to face her.

I said, Yes? She tugged my coat at the wrist and led me a step to the side, making room for a couple passing through the door. Catherine said, You didn't get my text?

I said, What? I wanted to ask her what she smelled and if her nostril hairs ever grew long enough to tug. Between our messages and their profile on the app, our roleplay interests overlapped neatly enough that I was terrified of disappointing them. Mother me meanly, I had texted. The two of them wrote back and informed me that I was using that word incorrectly. Which word they meant—*mother* or *meanly*—was never made clear to me. So excited by their correction, their attention as promised, I kept thinking, Be as mean as you promised you could be. With flesh Catherine in front of me, I was saying, What? I looked at her mouth—she was not smiling.

Catherine said, I sent you a text that we would wait for you outside. We saw you rush out of that car and when you blew by us, for a second, we weren't sure it was actually you. Above her narrowed eyebrows, a whitehead bloomed. I appreciated that she did not cover it for me.

So intense was both Catherine's calmness and my own shame that I could only apologize. Her hand still on the sleeve of my coat, she led me back to the table. I said, How did you recognize me? I hoped she might say they picked up on my terrible movement or bad blank aura.

You are exactly what you presented yourself as, she said. I turned my hand into a fist and pressed against her fingers clipped at my sleeve. She changed position to hold her wrist to my nose and instructed me to sniff. I did, embarrassed at my own eagerness, and when prompted, told her I smelled nothing.

Nothing, she said without looking at me. You're sure?

Skin, I said. I mean, good? Great? If she hit me in the

mouth my teeth could find a home in her skin. At least, I reasoned, until she knocked one loose.

She said, Good.

Katrina, bundled in a white coat with fur at its collar, held a mug in front of her chin as we approached. People seemed larger at their tables, seats pushed farther out, handbags and backpacks strewn about. I stepped carefully, watching for loose straps and umbrellas, while Catherine ambled ahead. I imagined tugging at the waistband of her jeans and ramming my hand into her underwear from behind. When she pulled a chair out for me I stopped short, stumbled over myself, and, with the wives watching me, sat and said, Thank you. Catherine did not acknowledge me with words, just a glance in my direction as she circled the table to sit beside her wife. Katrina lowered the mug, revealing a trio of red pimples. I imagined pressing pads of tea tree oil to the spots, observing, patiently, their journey to bulbs of white pus. Together, the three of us would burst them.

I could never bring myself to say a simple greeting in such situations. How does one say, Hi, there, when you have already seen one another's nipples? And so, my first words to Katrina were, Is your collar real fur?

She grinned. Her mouth was lopsided, bent toward the right. She said, Of course not, and fingered the collar. It's from H&M, last season.

We're vegan before six, Catherine said. We don't buy animal products like that. She took a long sip from a cold beverage, rattled the ice around, and sipped it again. She wore no gloves. Her hands were red, admitting one vulnerability none of us could sidestep: we were freezing. No humbling exists like a New England winter. The wives glanced at each other and back at me with set smiles.

You should try your coffee, Catherine said cheerfully and pushed the mug toward me. Though the coffee lapped around the edges, nothing spilled. I took the mug without touching her.

We asked for oat milk, Katrina said. They have a dairy option here, but we didn't want to risk it.

Right, of course, I said. I managed to look at their pleased faces and say, Thank you. I meant it. Catherine and Katrina read to me as attentive, perhaps in their steadiness, perhaps in their clearly agreed-upon desire to focus more on me than on each other, in an effort, I assumed, for us to feel like a tandem instead of a tricycle. These gestures—ordering coffee, considering potential dietary needs, though I myself had none—felt especially unfamiliar to me in the months after my parents committed their crime. Coverage in the local paper withheld the victim's name, though her age, eighty-six, made it clear to all in our community that the woman left to rot was my father's mother. If I came from such stock, who was I if not a brimful of evil to be moved away from with careful steps? I carried these shames whenever I met with couples, and whatever kindness they showed me was all the more pronounced because of this. I drank from the mug; the coffee burned my tongue and the top of my mouth. I winced and swallowed a second time.

No allergies, Catherine said. Cow's milk? Coconut? I

shook my head and she asked about peanuts latex sesame shellfish soy walnuts cashews almonds tomatoes and chestnuts. I kept shaking my head, feeling flattered, imagining them cooking for me already. When Catherine reached red meat mango dried fruit avocado and the pollen of birch trees I told them they'd have to try harder to kill me.

Gluten doesn't even bother me, I said. I'm a tank.

We're really glad you could make it, Katrina replied as though rehearsed. We were a little worried we scared you off, her wife added.

No, I said, pulling my face into pleasant. I really am sorry about the other day, when I bailed.

Remind me. You had a work thing come up, was it? Catherine spoke carefully, and I could sense she remembered quite clearly I had not given so specific of a reason.

More of a personal thing, I said. But it had nothing to do with you all. In truth, I had consumed a bottle of cough syrup and slept intermittently, content to continue avoiding the outside world after a day of working at home alone. The waitress from before fiddled with the dial of a mushroom heater maybe two feet from us.

What would you do, I said, if it tipped over? I directed this question toward Catherine, though both shook their head no.

Catherine said, You mean if it started a fire?

I said, Right. I was hopeful, awakened, and still cautious: they could be the sort of women who ran for the fire extinguisher, who pulled me out of the way, who rescued a baby.

They looked at each other. Don't get excited, Catherine said. She nodded at the water jugs and glasses stacked on an empty table to her side, previously missed in my peripheral vision. Nothing living would burn.

I shifted to asking what they would do if I inhaled propane. If there's a leak, I said.

The wives regarded each other. If you open it up, Katrina said to me, her face on Catherine's. If you put your mouth right on the lip?

Right, I said. Yes. I was thinking, Come on come on come come on come on.

We'd save you, Catherine said slowly, eyes still on her wife, the first of us three to smile. After about thirty seconds. Sixty seconds of inhalation, give or take, could kill a person, but half of that could be plenty of fun.

You wouldn't die, Katrina said. Is what she's getting at.

I believed—still believe—I could see their heat. I felt a fresh assurance that these women might be wonderful enough to hold me beneath water or leave me in dim woods. Brattiness came naturally to me; I never behaved that way as a girl and I wanted the same women who abandoned me to repair me.

I know what she means, I said, and we were all smiling then. Catherine cracked her wrists, a pleasant crinkle. I thought of my mother's pops and crackles; she taught my brother and me to release our bodies when we were still small enough to trust her. How funny she understood we ached even then.

I took another drink of the coffee before slipping a Dayquil from my pocket and placing it on my tongue. I drank it down hot hot hot. Catherine asked if I was contagious and I felt a thrill, a warmth, and offered my standard line: Just one of those colds. I imagined her offering to examine my throat and wondered how much of her face I could fit inside my jaw. Little, I figured, as my mouth is unusually narrow for an adult.

Catherine tapped her red fingers against her mug. Family? I remember you said you're from this area, aren't you? Her voice rang confident and cordial. No sign of the intimacy I thought we'd just established. She, I recalled, was from Connecticut, and Katrina, from coastal Maine.

No, I said, thinking of my parents in separate state correctional facilities. I checked inmate listings a few times a week. I was not yet at the point of obsession where I checked them daily. If my mother and father found me, my good self, my self that was sometimes described as sweet, if a bit taciturn, a bit strange, would turn catatonic. I could not control for every checkmate. I told the women, My family is from Massachusetts, but they don't come into the city. In light of the New Year, in light of mania, in light of hope, I named the town, a stretch of rocky coast with not one chain restaurant down its entire strip. I thought they would never remember it.

I miss my mother, Katrina said. I felt grateful for the shift in focus and surprised at her emotional astuteness. Ever since my dad passed, she continued, my mom's been so lonely. She's basically wasting away up there, all abandoned.

I told her I was sorry. Catherine kissed her forehead for a long moment and I did not look away, knowing I would want to remember and return to these seconds. Yes, Catherine loves Katrina. Yes, Katrina accepts Catherine's care. Yes, I bore witness to unity. I drank my coffee to its dregs and kept the cup in my hands. I shivered.

We lied, Katrina said.

I said, What?

Catherine faced her wife and said, You lied, actually.

I said, What?

It's not oat milk, Katrina said. It's almond.

I considered smashing my empty cup against my forehead. I can't tell, I said and looked at the wives. Their game was not yet clear to me, and why would it have been? I have only ever been the same girl who wanted her brain to be broken.

A waiter interrupted my stare, looking sheepish. He carried a wide white plate with a single pancake. I'm so sorry for the wait, he said. We're having a bit of a rush tonight.

Not a problem, Catherine answered for Katrina, who beamed at the food in front of her. The pancake oozed chocolate. In the center, a pile of melting whipped cream and two cherries.

When he turned, I asked, Do you add syrup to your pancakes?

Pan*cake*, Catherine corrected. I felt a pleasant sickness at finally receiving the sort of attention I craved with all couples before them: specific and mean. Her mind, I reasoned, could be nowhere but on me if she was able to notice a dropped plural. I thanked her and she tilted her face forward, eyebrows up, gray eyes bright.

Every table had a dish of very short sticks of very real butter. The maple syrup was contained in a short and thick jug. I passed the toppings to Katrina and said, Use both.

Katrina took a knife to the butter first. I always butter my carbs, she said, her laugh easy. Catherine confirmed this self-assessment with a nod. I was happy to watch them; obsession was a comfort, not a warning bell.

Katrina patted a neat line onto her pancake. That's not much butter, I said. I mean, for someone who loves it.

A silent communication transpired between the wives then, some sentiment expressed only through eye contact, and I recognized them as a couple with their own language. I understood then that Catherine and Katrina were equals at their core, unlike so many couples I had met before, who gave an air of constant dominance and submission. When the wives turned to face me, they did so in unison. I wanted to rupture the unity and to join it.

Your profile said you can take a little while to warm up, Katrina said, replacing the butter knife to the center of the table. And that's fine, because Catherine is the same way.

I'm soft once I'm comfortable, Catherine said. And you're the same, she said without looking at me. Or are you never?

I had the strong urge to piss my leggings. All of our quick caffeine. I wondered what the women would do. Catherine might gasp, embarrassed at her association with me, wondering what the patrons around us would think. Katrina I imagined screaming. The table might tilt but would not topple, as it was secured to the ground with locks. I held my bladder. I said, Am I never soft? I reminded myself to ask how often they pissed on each other in the shower.

No, Catherine said steadily. Are you never comfortable?

I am rarely comfortable, I said. Why else do you think I am chasing such an arrangement? The last word hung easy, as it always did.

She rattled her cup. The ice would take a long time to melt and become easier to swallow. So, she said, you're hoping to find a well-adjusted couple to help you feel better?

In more honesty, more New Year's gleam, I admitted I was looking for women to be kind to me by being mean, and to have sex with me, as well as breakfast. I said, I don't mention the good light in my bedroom to everyone, or for no reason. They looked triumphant. I was honest, but I was also testing them and myself. I made a game of seeing how little I could share and still keep a couple's interest, studying how much they projected onto me, their new little blank slate, and how much they cared when I inevitably disappeared. Of course, the wives could be playing their own game too.

I'm so happy we're sitting outside, Katrina said. I just wish we had more light.

Winters don't make it easy here, I said. To test Catherine's patience, I added, You two haven't considered Florida?

Catherine's laugh was a lull, Katrina's, a chortle. We actually bought our place in August, Catherine said. So we're getting comfortable here. She eyed me and added, And I'm not *that* old either, to head to Florida already. I remembered Katrina was a year or two younger than myself and Catherine, a good bit older but nothing shameful.

For now, Katrina said, and I watched her look at Catherine expectantly, as though reminding her of a line forgotten during a school play. They'd gone over this delicate language, I knew. What to share and what to withhold. Perhaps they were keeping my profile in mind. I specified I was looking for stable couples, no out-of-town types. No one whose wife or partner was away half the year, or every other weekend either. I felt if I could have one happiness in my choosing, it should be an entire bliss. Should be, should.

I tried to mimic Catherine's ease when I repeated, For now?

Catherine has some opportunities that might take us out of town, Katrina said carefully. But we don't know for sure yet.

It's unlikely, Catherine said. I mean, an honor, you know, but chances of it actually panning out are slim.

I couldn't shake the women I'd met in spite of my guidelines. One government librarian whose wife was an orthopedic surgeon at Mass General. Another whose live-in girlfriend was a public attorney for the incarcerated. Both couples offered one partner who was more attentive and available than the other, an imbalance I disliked. The couple I did not meet because the busy wife was a girl I'd grown up with and briefly dated in the past: Amy. The woman who knew about my tired parents and my dead brother. She messaged me that we didn't have to go back to the past, didn't have to get heavy, but I blocked their account. I didn't want anyone who knew my history to watch me disappear into myself. Less than two years later, I heard from the wives.

Catherine kissed Katrina's forehead again, eyes open and up, as though assessing her joy against the size of thick evening clouds, and I thanked them for telling me. I even added that this complication did not have to be a problem. I asked, Where would it take you?

Vermont, Katrina answered with Catherine's lips again going to her hairline. A source of comfort for the both of them, I guessed. I said it was not terribly far. I thought of the Amtrak and the buses and the app I used for rental cars to visit my grandmother.

And not terribly close, Catherine added.

And you, I said to Katrina. You would work remotely, or what?

I'd have to quit, technically, and see if I got hired back when we got home, she said. We'd be away three or four months, at most.

When I asked where she worked they answered simultaneously; Catherine said, Retail, while Katrina said, I sell shoes. They laughed again, Catherine's jaw only minimally widened and Katrina's mouth a slim oval, and after forming and closing the roundness of her mouth a few times Katrina said, I work at a sports clothing store on Newbury Street. I named one, and was wrong, then tried again, and they nodded together.

It's not much, Katrina said, but at least I can choose my schedule. She looked around, beyond me, as though checking to see if her store manager was lingering about. I shared that I worked weekends sometimes too. I felt my familiar, special delight in not elaborating on what my side job was. And, too, I wanted to test, test, test.

Lots of overtime? Catherine asked. Katrina looked at Catherine instead of at me and so I withheld.

Not quite, I said. I put the mug to my mouth and tongued it again, still empty. I said, It's really more of a volunteer gig.

The women watched me longer, then kissed. I learned my first punishment for withdrawing from them and asked

Katrina if she liked selling shoes. I wondered if Catherine was strong enough to lift me, decided she wasn't, but still imagined her holding me up by the armpits, like I'd seen parents do with children at the park. Katrina would lie faceup on the floor and lick the underside of my feet, eyes open and tongue long, Catherine's orders, upsetting us both and pleasing her wife.

I like helping people, Katrina said. Being useful. She closed her eyes and said, I bet we're in the running with a lot of others. Aren't we? Her voice revealed an insecurity that excited me.

I surprised myself at my clarity, my ability to say what I felt without prearrangement. I said, Not really, no.

Catherine watched Katrina chew, then faced me, making quick work of examining the both of us, perhaps to show me what she would be capable of handling later, should the situation call for it. She said, I would have thought a lot of people would have messaged you.

You're rare, Katrina said. A unicorn.

Especially because you don't want men, Catherine said. Isn't that right, no men?

That's right, I said. No men. Eager to flip the attention from me, I asked if they had sought a third before. I added a cough, wondering which answer would offer me comfort.

The wives took my question in stride. We have, Catherine said, but not quite like this. When I realized Catherine and Katrina had ignored my cough, I added another. Still dry, still from the cap of my lungs.

Katrina said, We've met a few women at parties. We tried

one kink event, but it ended up being mostly gay men. She said, Are you sick?

Yes, Catherine said. On antibiotics, is it? That's why we didn't meet for a drink.

No, I said, thrilled once more by their attentiveness. Just a tickle.

The wives appeared nonplussed. And of course, your listing, Catherine said. The women from before were not quite so involved. Katrina nodded, as though their thoughts permeated from the same center. The meetings, the calls.

I rolled the rim of the mug against my bottom lip. I said, I know I ask for a lot.

It's a good way of weeding people out, Katrina said brightly. Catherine kissed her temple. I imagined separating her hair from its scalp. I felt slighted by their intimacy and could not help but ask, Does she get an A, professor? Catherine laughed but a sharpness in her glare served its purpose; she did not want to be teased, I understood, and yet these tests were entirely normal for me, entirely necessary. Katrina looked thrilled at this back-and-forth and said, Everything we do is always changing everything.

Catherine and I repeated in unison, Everything?

Yes, everything, Katrina said. Crossing the street at one block instead of another. Or answering a call instead of listening to the voicemail a few minutes later. Opening a shift instead of closing. These decisions are small, sometimes automatic, but they really do spiral out.

Do they? I could not resist. Catherine mmed in support of her wife but appeared amused.

Katrina's excitement sped with our attention. Think about it, she directed, and I confess, I did. We're all working, right? Busy, trying to get whatever task it is done. And there's personal pressure, and then there's capitalism, of course, and money, and hours. And if we didn't work that day, well, we might lose the job entirely, or get a bad review, and lose it down the road. Okay, we know that. But imagine if we— here she looked at Catherine, though I of course knew that I was not yet part of a *we*—had both worked today, or even late yesterday, and we decided well, we're a bit tired, and after all you—here they both looked at me, as I was of course the separate *you*—had canceled once before, even though we'd both arranged our work around that meeting, so, imagine if we had said, maybe even sensibly, well, I need to work, and so that's that.

You wouldn't have met me, I said. I pressed my napkin to my mouth and jerked my shoulders forward, as though swallowing a lick of stomach brine. I understood the first boundary: don't shrug off their attention; don't waste their time.

At that Catherine said she would get the check. I moved to get my wallet, zippered into the good pocket of my coat, and Catherine, as I expected she might, said, No, no, you can get it the next time. I smiled and opened my mouth to thank her and she reached one hand out, fingers cupped as though to hug my neck, and I leaned into her. I was thinking, Here? Could I be so lucky. But she only flicked my jugular and said I had a crumb. I didn't, of course; I hadn't eaten a bite, but I thought I'd passed a kind of test by moving toward her instead of away.

With Catherine gone, the table went silent, and I wondered if Katrina might go for my neck or ribs or get down beneath the table and put her head between my legs. Instead, she pointed out that I'd had my drink without asking a thing about it. You drank it right down, she said. We could have put anything in it.

Sure, I said. Poison?

We don't love you, Katrina said. Not yet. Her chin stuck out in a determined way before she said it, and I would later learn this motion was a tic of hers to appear certain and mature.

I laughed but was thinking about how to earn their love, how to get poisoned, how to get sick. These wants were not new, but I was thrilled not to initiate, to avoid the humiliating process of explaining my desires. Women would tell me, *sure, I'm game to try it*, or, *well, have you done this before, don't lie*, or, *I'll put poison control on speed dial, ha ha*, and I could always tell they were debating if I was really beautiful enough to be worth this sort of risk and the answer was always no in the end. To test Katrina, I told her about my camming.

I said, When I was in college, I supported myself and my parents. Helping them pay their phone bills, stuff like that.

Katrina leaned toward me, doubled over her skinny belly, amused. My sophomore year, I continued, surprising and scaring myself, the friend of a classmate I was dating told me she made money selling photos of her feet on this website. I checked it out. Not bad, basically what you'd expect. Instead of the photos, I went for live streams. Just my feet, nothing too hard or too terrible. A few nights a week, sometimes while my girlfriend and I watched TV in her dorm room. I tried to keep myself from smiling, as I did not want Katrina to think I was opening up a joke about her job. Though miserable in my circumstances, those nights watching baking competitions in our sweatpants while I made some money were actually quite good. Bliss where you accept it, and all that.

Katrina said, You were camming, you mean? I heard curiosity and a glimmer of something new: interest, or desire. I thought of her wife, who I imagined was the sort of woman who would pay for her pornography and consider it redistributing her wealth. I released a cough without covering my face. Katrina did not pull back. I told her she had been contaminated and she smiled.

I said yes. Making money from camming is more competitive now, I think. I don't know, I haven't tried since law school. I continued on with the story of my life and said, I have a private social media account where I stream my feet for women. No money, no monthly payments, no sign-ups. I chat with some women. Once in a while, I'll meet one or two or three. I tell some dates and when they log in to watch they alert me over text, usually with a nude, and I'll drop them a special hello into the general stream: *hello, doctor, hello, is the library quiet, hello, hi, A, hey, you, what's the political scandal of the day.* Women love shout-outs because it makes them feel exclusive, memorable. I love giving them because it made me feel in control. I never show my face or tell my name. I wanted to ask if she was shocked, repulsed, delighted, or all three, but stopped when I felt her wife's hand on my shoulder.

Come to dinner when we invite you. With a kiss to my

forehead, she muttered to bring my feet. And then, her face like a fox's, she said, I got you something special. She placed a brown box in front of me and later, alone in my apartment, I would open it to find one pancake. Staring up at me, chocolate chips formed eyes and a round mouth, screaming, screaming. In pleasure or fear, I could not tell. I hoped Catherine made a special request, that she gave detailed instructions to the cashier, perhaps, even that she sent one pancake back and requested the face to be redone. Not too happy, she might have said. And not so obviously afraid. After eating I refused to brush my teeth, letting the sugar sit in me as long as I could keep it, a little control of my own to balance what I sensed I was about to give up.

3

THE OFFICE SMELLED OF WINTER FLOW-
ers. I did not grow up using such scents, nor
thought to involve them in my own home, but I
had learned the name for the earthy, easy scent that filled my
nostrils and then my brain and then my reproductive organs
after stopping into a janitorial supply closet to film my feet in
the early days of my employment. I got the interview and eventually an offer, my only job offer after months of interviews,
thanks to a lesbian I went to law school with; we weren't close,
but she told me she was worried about me and knew of an
opening at her previous firm, so she passed my name along to
human resources. With twenty-six floors and a bloated staff
filled with men eager to both have ideas and take credit for
them, my feet embraced a world of opportunity. Finding the
office's nooks and crannies recharged me. Understand I did
not then believe I would be of any interest to my coworkers,
especially not enough to be followed.

That cold winter day I went into my regular stall—direct
middle of the row of three—kicked my shoes off, live streamed
my feet, and released a long line of piss. Women on the app

told me they were happy to see me, they loved me, they missed me all morning. Someone offered to pick me up and drive me wherever I needed to go before the storm. Someone else asked if I ever did full-frontal shots. My favorite message of the day included a woman telling me she timed her bathroom breaks with mine so she wouldn't miss a moment; *it's my version of self-care*, she wrote. I responded to only her that day and said, *I love you always, my little feminist.* I heard footsteps and listened for the click of a stall lock. I pulled my pants up without wiping and exited the stall to find Emma rubbing baby powder into her bangs.

Emma Emma Emma. Technically my inferior, Emma hovered. Despite graduating from the local Ivy, Emma did not seem to understand hints. Social cues were lost on her, even from me, even in the months I stopped bothering with deodorant or wearing underwear beneath my slacks. Emma, the sort of woman who still wore a watch and checked it, liked to make herself useful—and be in everyone's way—by cleaning the coffee maker on a schedule only she adhered to, people trying to get a cup before client meetings be damned.

You're so regimented, Emma told me once I was beside her at the sink. She did not wash her hands as I did. I asked her what she meant. I had been thinking about the wives—I wanted to film a little something for them later, using my toes to spell their names in the grime on my shoes.

Always in here at the same time, she said with a smile. Robotic. Her eyes did not leave me when I hit the air dryer into action with my elbow.

I said, Coffee makes me piss. I pushed my hands up to the

vent and was disappointed to find the air was barely warm. I wondered if the wives washed each other's hands and if they'd let me into the rotation. If both tested her fingers in my mouth, I figured, Katrina's would smear lotion onto my tongue and Catherine would be sure suds lingered on her knuckles. If I managed to make her just the right amount of mad, I hoped she would wash with dish soap.

Emma said, Sometimes you don't pee. I made my mouth a circle, then a line and wondered, Does she know? I told her I seized up when I heard anyone else. I tried for the single stall, I lied, aware I was saying too much, making my behavior all the more suspicious. Her face shone with confidence as if she had me arranged on her living room wall, all glass-eyed and wooden-toothed. As I wiped my hands, still damp, on the front of my slacks, she told me to take better care of myself. She said, Holding it can make you sick. At my silence, she added that she loved my shoes. A warning, a missive. In her eyes, I briefly saw: I love you. When the door shut behind her, I vowed to flirt with her at least a little less, foster a little more distance.

Emma, a bisexual and eager to discuss it with me, the only out lesbian in the office. I imagine her interest in me stemmed from this. Perhaps the smell of my dry shampoo, all coconut and salt water, made her feel comfortable detailing her Thursday nights at one of the grungier drag king shows in the city. Sounds like you were the bell of the ball, I would tell her after she described free drinks and phone numbers and being brought on stage. Sounds like you were the prettiest girl in the place. She'd glow but stand stiff, like her programming hadn't given her a full range of emotional responses. I tried to flirt with restraint; I wasn't trying to get fired over her. But she also seemed to possess an awareness that she could ruin me with only a little focus. That's how I rationalized her appearing in the women's restroom a touch too often. Why she often watched me wash my hands.

My hands were still damp when my mother called post-Emma. She was early, which surprised and concerned me—I always worried she was going to mouth off and be put in isolation. I knew I wouldn't be my mother's first choice of comfort, but given her inability to call my father, I couldn't imagine who else she would turn to in a time of real danger. I answered from a favorite filming closet.

No women—not Catherine and Katrina, not even Emma and her peculiarities—shifted the regularity with which I answered my mother's calls. The calls typically came between six and eight on Tuesday and Thursday and I answered them regardless of where I was: on the train home, on foot, in a shared car with colleagues. As a child, I longed for this degree of stability from my mother. How I wanted her to pick me up from school on the days I missed the bus, taking too long to wipe in the bathroom, chatting with a friend who stayed late for softball, sometimes waiting to watch my sophomore-year algebra teacher meet her rumored partner in the school parking lot. Notice my absence, and prove you love me.

A voice informed me I was receiving a call from the state women's corrections facility. The voice was not my mother's; I thought of it as a robot's voice, but that wasn't true either. A woman had recorded the message letting me know about the charges. She might have practiced. She might have asked for rewrites for the sake of musicality. She might be getting royalties. This thought made me happy: a woman getting the most for doing little.

Hi, I said from the closet. Hi, hi, hi. I started saying hi before the call connected because I knew my mother wouldn't hear it until we both heard the click. Like always, my mother said her own name, not *mom*, or *mother*, or *mama*, but her first name. I accepted the call.

As always, I heard quiet until another recording popped on, alerting us that we had reached the two-minute mark, then one minute, then thirty seconds—unless we added more time—then silence.

4

MY FATHER, ON THE OTHER HAND, TALKED the whole time we spent on the phone. His calls were less regular than my mother's, more frequent when he needed money, and less frequent when he was bitter I was not giving or doing enough. No, I would not pay for a private attorney when he was assigned a public defender. No, as I reminded him again and again, I could not represent him. No, I did not want to write or give a statement relaying a belief that he deserved to get out early.

My most recent boundary was that I would not see him in person if he was going to keep asking me to do him *that favor*, as he called it, a character statement, which I understood as lying. My father, of course, realized I would be his best shot at an early release; if even I, his remaining child and an attorney myself, believed he deserved early autonomy, a judge might think longer about the recovering addict in front of him. Character statements can be important or meaningless depending on the judge, the case, and, unfairly, the positionality of the person who writes them. We both knew this. But what I did not describe to my father was my obsessive want to see him and my mother learn. Not from me, but from the world. I did not think they deserved freedom, a second chance, a real shot at happiness, not when he left his own mother alone for so long that her skin stuck to her reclining chair, her urine and feces forming a connective layer of rot.

And still, my father evaded responsibility. He held firm to the belief that it was really my mother's job to check in on his mother, while he was out and about. That's how he put it: out and about. Perhaps if his evasion did not remind me quite so much of the first accident, the first family loss, the first tragedy, I would not want so badly to hear his apology, to see it, to feel it. Such was my sense of justice in those years: little restorative, much revenge. And so, still, my anger.

On the phone, men in the background yelled, though the other inmates fought less than I anticipated. Or at least, it seemed that way when they were close to using their phone privileges. No one wants to lose right at the end. Mostly the men gassed one another up. The more my father held the phone inches from his mouth and shouted, It's my daughter, hey, hey, the more men yelled that I'm his hot piece, his little bitch, his girl back home.

Hel, he said the day after I saw the wives.

I said, Yeah? I sat on my floor and sorted laundry as we spoke. When I bunched my socks—mostly matching pairs, as they were all faded white anyway—I thought of Katrina's affinity for serendipity. If I hung my shirts by color, would my choices change the outset of my day? A cream blouse instead of white leading to a life revived. I rolled my underwear into a ball after I checked for tears in the crotch lining. I put the balled pair into my mouth and wondered how quick the wives were with rope.

My father said, Hel, I have a good feeling.

I removed the underwear from my mouth. I said, Whatever you're thinking, remember this is a monitored line. I added a laugh to assuage whoever was listening. Just father and daughter, joking, as they do.

Ha, he said, not really laughing. Too focused for that. Hel, I've been thinking about my life in chunks. You know, with age.

I said, Uh huh. I tugged a loose thread at the base of a sweater until it unraveled all the way around. I said, Dad, is this what we talked about before?

His sigh came through the phone as an echo. Eager, like a whisper, he said, Did you think about it?

I told him I could hang up anytime. The last time my father asked me to submit a character statement for his parole hearing, I immediately thought, No. I had said, I'll think about it. Being yelled at over the phone should have been easier to swallow, just a click and it goes away, but the panicked feeling stayed with me each time I refused to help. Now I said, You never give me what I want.

He said, Hel, honey. I don't know what you mean. I gave him silence and he said, About my mom, huh? And he was both wrong and right; I wanted answers about my dead brother and my nearly dead grandmother. I wanted answers about myself but I didn't know how to ask the questions.

I said, Dad. I told him to say it but I still don't know what the *it* was, not really.

He tried to make himself human to me and told me he felt like shit about what happened to his mom every day. I saw the pictures, he added. From the hospital.

I imagined the photos of my grandmother many times. Physicians took them, or more likely, nurses. Residents, maybe. Learning how to focus the flash on a festered wound. How to angle the shot so the stages of decay are clear for the pathologists. Evidence of their treatment for the state insurance company, their long hours of work. No hospital wants to be scapegoated when the body needs to speak for the victim. If she did not survive the infections, the dehydration, the heat, there would be investigations into my parents and what proof would police have? Pus and rot. I like to believe the photos were acts of love too. Darling, they might have said to her as she slept with her morphine drip, You don't need to remember a thing. We've got it here, all right? I imagined a staff of people in blue scrubs and white coats kissing her forehead. Rest now. Rest.

He asked if I had seen them and I said no. Without asking if I wanted to hear it, he described bed sores on her lower back, thighs, and calves. Sores had blossomed on the tops of her feet too.

Her feet, I said, frowning. I admitted to him I didn't know she was diabetic. I thought of her puddings and sips of liquor. Did she wear an insulin pump? I never dressed her. I only dressed the doll. What else didn't I see? What else didn't I realize.

No, my father said. I guess irritation, from her . . . From her mess—you know what I mean. It stayed on her skin and really irritated it. He said, The sores turned green.

Right, I said, remembering an article described her as having been found sitting in her excrement. I imagined skinless toes. My mind horrified me. I needed a distraction from the hurt of the living. I shifted to Ryan. I reminded my father they never talked about my brother with me, ashamed of the emotion in my voice.

He told me I could always ask my mother, and even laughed, and I found myself laughing too. I think he and I shared the same happy anger.

I said, I guess we both want things we can't have, then. He was quiet, though I heard rustling behind him, reassurance that he hadn't vanished. His voice changed—lower, I think, maybe even hurt—and he asked if I was serious, if I really was making his life so damn bad just because I had an idea stuck in my head. I told him yes, I was serious, and if he wanted my help so badly, he could help me for once. I hadn't intended to draw a line between us but found myself agreeing with my points as I spoke: Who was he to demand an act of love when we hardly tolerated each other's living?

You'd help me out with the statement, he said, if we talked about him?

I said, Yeah, though I wasn't sure. My mind opened with everything I wanted to know, and I felt, too, an absolute certainty that neither of my parents could give me what I really wanted: the warmth of the boy beside me on the floor, picking each other's snot, giggling, before one of us got better and the other got sicker.

Come, he said. Spend the anniversary with me. I mhmmed, though we'd never done this, even when he wasn't incarcerated.

I knew my brother's death date was coming up, though I could never remember the precise day. Only the highlights: January, little sunlight, heat cut off, oven on and open for warmth, socks on our hands while we slept. We never talked about Ryan, so he'd become more myth than boy. I questioned if my father knew the date and loved him just enough not to ask.

He said, I know you want answers but it's gotta be in person.

You'll tell me what I want to know, I said, if I promise to write the statement?

Promise, he repeated, too slow. You aren't a kid, Helen.

I said, What?

He said, I don't give nobody shit for a promise. You do it or you don't.

On the phone, I worked through strange thoughts. My dad might love me. If I write the damn statement, he might write my mother and tell her I was being good to our family, that I was taking care of him and, maybe in the future, even her. He might make the dead boy alive in memories. I could be a good girl to them. But the family in my thoughts was still my family: dead boy and almost-dead old woman. When I told my father to eat shit, I was thinking of vengeance, of loyalty to my fellow weak ones. I was thinking I didn't need blood to understand myself, that I was reborn in my sex and my cough syrup and my compulsions.

I hung up on my father as he told me to fuck myself, and I kept that high until I saw the wives not once but twice more— until they asked a question no one had, until they made me accept ghosts bear weight.

5

THE THREE OF US LASTED JUST UNDER one week apart. In the time between the cafe and our next meeting, them picking me up at my building's cross streets—I did not give them my exact address—I swayed between messaging them at Catherine's number and ignoring their messages for hours. Rapid absenting. We exchanged a number of nudes, complimenting one another's bodies and aesthetics. I took care to include my feet in many and a cough syrup cap in one, though they did not address either. Well, I thought on the sidewalk. We shall see.

The wives stopped their car at the corner. The car's gray resembled how I experienced most winter days: bleak and too bright to face head-on. But that January day was easy, whimsical to witness if not to live. I hurried to the corner, ice be damned, believing that if I tumbled, I could watch them evaluate how to care for me. I did not fall.

Catherine was at the wheel, Katrina in the front seat, both unbuckled and with their faces in each other's hair. I said hello and buckled then unbuckled myself, feeling idiotic. They ignored me and I listened to their deep breaths, the great languish of their respective throats, and imagined hurling myself into the middle of traffic.

Do you like cherry blossoms, Katrina said without looking at me, or green melon?

To eat? I was imagining licking pink petals from trees in a city like D.C. or Seattle, both places I had never been.

The scents, Catherine said without laughing. We're always surprising each other with new smells.

Come on, Katrina said. They were both pulling their hair up and giggling. Give us a sniff.

From my place in the middle of the back seat, I put my face between their heads and they leaned in. I hoped they might smother me but they only stayed still long enough for me to take one two three four deep breaths. I smelled something. Vague shampoo or grease or sunscreen. I said, Um.

They said, Guess.

I said, Katrina has the blossoms and Catherine the melon.

They said, You're sure?

I said, Well.

They drew away from each other and from me and Catherine started the car. We both used vanilla shampoo, she said. But don't worry about it. They chuckled together and ignored me for the rest of the drive. I wanted to put my torso out of the window like a dog. See me again, I was thinking. When I removed my seatbelt, the car dinged. Don't do that, Catherine said, and I buckled myself back in.

The drive to the reservoir was less than twenty minutes, during which I worried about the shampoo and watched the sidewalks in case my father appeared. Guilt kept him in my mind, and I worried about the conditions of whatever jail van he was trotted around in once or twice a year for court. Let me guess, I said to Katrina as we pulled into a parking spot on the street, Catherine doesn't let you drive unless she's drunk? I wanted to regain some control, or at least see what they would do if I tried to be smart.

Catherine and Katrina gave each other that look from the cafe again.

I actually don't drive, Katrina said. She unbuckled and turned to look directly at me. I never learned.

I'm teaching her, Catherine said. She parallel parked in two tries. Do you want to tell her?

I finally passed the test to get my permit, Katrina said, so now it's just the driving hours and the exam. Her cheeks revealed her vulnerability. I worried people taunted her. I'm terrified to go places without Catherine anyway, she added. I was curious to know if she would seek a substitute driver during her wife's end-of-the-semester rush but was afraid to hear the answer. I picked up a picnic basket the wives had packed and told her I understood.

The wives held hands and kept me in the middle, two steps ahead of them, so we formed a sort of triangle on the dirt walking path. We made slow time around the water in one loop, none of us wanting to be the one to complain about the cold. At the sound of footsteps, one woman and her unleashed dog, I imagined my mother, walking a dog she had perhaps stolen from a stranger's yard. None of us shared a hello but the wives and I moved to the side and offered room, a gentler, better greeting. Catherine identified the tree-tapping of a downy woodpecker. Katrina swore she saw the black streak of a chickadee. I knew no birds.

We stopped at a gazebo so they could spread the checkered blanket Catherine had in her purse. Around us, sugar maples stood without their leaves. Across the water, red pines showed off their colors.

The wives ate the dairy four hours before their nightly cutoff.

Catherine spread wet warm cheese on the chunks of bread Katrina handed her. I watched them and kept my gloves on until Catherine said, Here, and passed me a real plate. The white porcelain felt heavy and cool. I traced my fingers along the painted blue flowers that lined the edge. From your kitchen, I said, and they said, Yes, together.

We try to avoid plastic, Katrina said. You know.

I thought of the trays of frozen food in my freezer, the miniature bags of chips and cookies I kept at my desk in the office. My life, a reusable waste. I said, Definitely.

Catherine said, Eat, and though I wanted to test her, to press against a simple order, I put the bread and cheese and red jam into my mouth.

Raspberry, Katrina said. Wonderful, isn't it?

I said, The best, and tried to cover my mouth while I chewed. When the wives smirked at each other I felt sure I was being made a fool and repeated raspberry. Together they corrected, Marionberry. They appeared delighted.

I don't think I have your taste buds, I said. The gene that makes food really intense or whatever.

You don't, they said.

Makes it all too easy to mess with my food, I said, still chewing, bread wet in the side of my mouth. I was expecting them to laugh, but they only looked at each other.

You don't know us at all, Catherine said, if you think we want anything to be easy. Then Katrina asked me about my favorite beach.

Before I replied, Catherine added, In Massachusetts, specifically.

I said, Um. I asked if she meant on the Cape or what. I knew they'd already been to Provincetown from their photos and felt unsettled. Surely, I thought, they're already in the know about the local beaches? Catherine told me no, she was curious if I was familiar with the south or north shore. They kept their faces on me, relaxed and curious. Katrina showed no surprise at all, no thinking, only pure, easy anticipation.

I told the wives I did not have a favorite. Not entirely a lie: the stretch of beach I'd grown up on was not a favorite. It was a rocky coast best admired when dressed in snow; I could not describe it as a destination to go out of one's way for. My positive memories were all pies from the grocery store eaten with sand-crusted fingers and my parents holding me under waves until they deemed me ready to be brought up for air. My brother must have been there too, kicking and punching water, seaweed taking root beneath his suit, happy and surprised when brought above water to realize he was still, at least for that moment, alive. Understand these are memories I cannot tell a person, much less two.

Katrina told Catherine they should perhaps be more direct. The couple wrinkled their noses at each other and, worried I smelled, I cleared my throat, which they ignored. In the distance, a woodpecker seemed to laugh at us, or more likely, at me. I said I agreed with Katrina, that they should just say it. Catherine told me it was important to her to keep Katrina safe, and so she does a lot of Googling. She asked me if I understood and I told her sure. I considered bolting for the woods and yet their focus compelled me.

We looked into you, Catherine said. And it was all fine, obviously. But we learned about some people, some relatives we thought might be yours, and we were wondering if you knew anything about it. Katrina moved to hold Catherine's hand. I rested both of mine on my thighs as I did not want to risk hitting either of their faces or my own. I mhmmed and Catherine told me they'd done some digging and found a woman who shared my last name, who lived in a town that matched what I'd described at the cafe, and who did a very bad thing.

The family nature made the crime all the more haunting and intriguing to outsiders. Drug abuse and overdoses were not uncommon in our stretch of seaside Massachusetts, but elder neglect rang differently. People at the one supermarket in town talked: What were my parents thinking? Did they want her to starve to death? There was talk that they'd left a weapon in hopes she'd die by suicide but I knew my parents were uneasy around guns. Someone messaged me on Facebook; she said we'd gone to high school at the same time but I didn't recognize her, all pregnant next to an ugly man in her photos. I heard you found her, she wrote. Sooo sorry!!! I wondered if Amy started that rumor and couldn't blame her.

A YouTuber with a few hundred subscribers pontificated on what was really to be gained from her suffering: My parents already received her social security checks, didn't they? Why not sign her up for Meals on Wheels and let her live comfortably? A commenter said addicts don't make sense and someone else replied and said this went beyond addiction: Had these people been evaluated for personality disorders? I searched similar channels for months but no one else covered the case. I considered offering more information to users with big platforms, on one condition: Explain it to me. Make me understand what I don't.

Even before my parents were found guilty in a case a local reporter described as the stuff of *Lifetime* movies, my parents were both on probation for driving a car that was unregistered and uninsured (my mother) and for carrying a soda bottle cap, several damp cotton balls, and a shoelace, all of which contained just a bit of heroin, in said car (my father). That's how he put it to me, later: just a bit, just a bit.

The state's district attorney brought forward the charges of elder neglect, and from what I read, tried valiantly, but with the victim unable, or unwilling, to testify, there wasn't much movement. So, the judge, the plea, the deal. My father received a longer sentence because of his record, but I would have resented him more than my mother regardless, as I felt that should he love just one person more than himself, it should have been his mother, not his partner. I myself never appeared at court proceedings: guilt, guilt.

Had I visited my grandmother at home, I might have been able to speak on her behalf. I might have borne witness to neglect before it got so bad—before the sores took root. I might have made the phone call to the police instead of Amy, innocent Amy, just trying to show me she cared about my family, or at least took pity on my grandmother. The universe might have spun out in ways my slight brain could not derive. But I stayed away, drinking shit beer and fingering strange women. Calling myself empowered in estrangement.

At the picnic with the wives, I asked if we looked alike.

There's no picture, Katrina said. Like, no mug shot. Catherine said she wasn't sure if newspapers had stopped running things like that. Katrina added that it was totally barbaric, the way people's faces can be ruined before they're proven guilty. I said I agreed, though I did not, and asked what they wanted to know.

Do you know that woman, or the man? Her boyfriend, Catherine said. She said my mother's name and fumbled over my father's. I danced my nails into the beds of my fingers and counted backward from ten twice before I told them my parents never married and Katrina said, So those are your parents? And I nodded.

Together they said, Oh.

I said, Oh? I worked my thumbnail into the nail bed of my pointer finger on the opposite hand and unearthed fresh flesh. I suckled at the blood and felt both relieved I had not fled and furious with myself. I thought of myself as stupid, foolish, a waste, a joke for letting these women figure out a thing about me. And yet I felt brave too, on the brink of a change. I wondered if this was what people meant when they described a fresh start, a new you, a new me.

So, Catherine said. You don't have your father's last name?
I told her she was right, I have my mother's. I told them most
people probably did not connect me to the people in that article, if they searched for me at all. The name is not so unusual
in an area with many third- and fourth-generation Irish families; had I been smarter, less open, had I not named the town
I was from when Catherine pressed at the cafe, she might not
have made the connection, might have only read about my
parents and their elder abuse trial in the court section of a
local paper and thought, Oh, Jesus Christ. But I did and they
did too.

The wives waited and I informed them my mother thought
it was a very feminist act not to get married and my father's
name, in fact, wasn't even on my birth certificate. They waited
longer and I added that my father technically had a warrant
out when my mother was giving birth, and so they decided
to just add his name later, to avoid the hospital notifying the
police—he was fucked up, I'd been told, and so the paranoia
was high—but within the window of time one can update
such a document for free, they forgot. I did not tell the wives
that, for the sake of making our family less confusing, Ryan
also had my mother's last name, though I believe my father
was only high at his birth, not also avoiding small-town police
over a missed parole meeting.

The wives said, Oh. Katrina said I must miss my parents
very much. I looked away until the wives, in unison, balanced
forward on their knees. They kissed either side of my face.
This action could not have been planned, I told myself, and yet
I felt certain it was. This notion comforted me. I told them I

missed having a family but I did not know how to share space with any person. They nodded, although I sensed they did not understand.

Were you close before the whole thing with your grand-mother happened? Catherine said. I noticed you weren't named in any of the articles.

Yeah, Katrina said. None of the coverage mentioned children.

I told them I had been estranged. Like all people upon hearing that word, their faces revealed a morbid interest. Because we were cold, and because they had kissed me, and because I wanted to receive their obsessive interest as a com-pliment, I told them I'd cut my parents off when they devel-oped a habit of both asking me for money and yelling at me. I was in college, I said, and I guess they didn't know how to keep living and paying for their shit without me at home to help out. The wives nodded and I sensed they were intention-ally looking only at me, not at each other, and I again wanted to know if they talked through this ahead of time. Did one of them close the laptop after reading about my parents late into the night and say, Jesus, when we press this out of her, we have to go full therapist, no judgment, no bad jokes? I thought Katrina might care more about my feelings, about how deeply this would shame a person, and yet in Catherine's expression I saw an increased desire to consume me. I understood both responses, of course, as versions of love. I explained I paid for stuff until I got tired of all their voicemails, the fighting, the meanness when I didn't reply quickly enough or hustle to the Western Union at night. I said, I couldn't afford their habits.

The wives said, Uh huh. Catherine asked if it had been a long time between cutting them off and finding out about what they did to my grandmother. I admitted my boundaries were shaky at best; they'd get a friend to email me on their behalf, or they'd find my address from a cousin and send me a handwritten letter, and I'd do what they wanted: send money, solve a problem, tell them I was sorry for whatever. Within a year of my biggest, longest no, I found the article that detailed their arrest.

No one called you when they found your grandmother? Catherine said. For the first time, she appeared to doubt my story.

My impulse was to lie, as I always did, bury Amy and her goodness, but I was enamored with the wives, with their attention and their prodding, and so I said yes, actually, a woman I was seeing told me; we'd grown up together, I said, and it was a coincidence she was in town, had decided to stop by. The wives asked questions, of course: What was her name, why did you split up, where is she now and what did she see, exactly? I got her name out and gave myself a silent congratulations for being brave. And stopped there.

In truth, when Amy wandered into my grandmother's house, with a hot pie in her hands, she found her small body closer to death than not. Amy called. We talked. I said, What, what, what, what, and she said my name over and over. I wouldn't find out about the arrests until later, alone on the internet.

Perhaps if the wives had been holding my hands or had told me to rest my head across their laps, I would have told them about my inability to maintain even a casual intimacy with Amy once I knew what she knew. But they were not, and did not, so instead, I asked the wives if they would tell me if one of them died and they looked at each other before saying, Sure.

I asked the wives to tell me something about their families. Katrina told me her father didn't always live with them, that her parents had what was described as a rough patch a few summers in a row. He had been drinking, she said, until he stopped. Catherine told me she ate her twin while in the womb. Katrina told her wife to be more honest, to just tell me, and I felt an incredible curiosity, back to childhood even, when I watched classmates share tubes of ChapStick between them, lips frosted coconut and cherry, bearing witness to an understanding that existed both without me and in front of me. I perked my face right up, hoping to appear interested without spooking Catherine's potential honesty away.

I was married before Katrina, Catherine said. At my silence, she continued: My ex left me because I was a bitch in my early thirties, I guess. Katrina added that Catherine was never a *bitch*, but that she used to be quite a control freak. Manipulative, Catherine said, then added she'd mostly outgrown it. I asked Catherine how she met Katrina and they gave each other a look, not as an understanding but as a weighing, deciding in real time how to handle my small, ordinary question. Katrina finally said they'd met while Catherine was tutoring her and a handful of other dancers to take the GED. I left high school to join a second company, Katrina said. And I never got my diploma, so I decided on a whim to take the test, not realizing, obviously, I'd forgotten every damn thing about school.

I said, Ah. I said, Catherine was your teacher? The slight scandal of their dynamic intrigued me; I'd sensed that Catherine had a desire to prove herself superior, but had not expected them to meet in this sort of environment. I was riled up, invigorated. I wondered how my role with them might shift if I stuck around—or if they followed me.

Catherine informed me there were no explicit rules, as everyone in those classes was over eighteen and not enrolled in a formal degree-seeking program. She let me know it wasn't as though Katrina were one of her undergraduates, not like she came to office hours and anything happened. Beside her, Katrina gave me a coy look. I wondered if this was a lie, a test to see how I would react to Catherine, if I might consider her a predator or a creep or otherwise alarming. She appeared proud and content and a little angry. I comforted myself with the idea that if I pushed her, she would take me by the shoulders or the throat and demolish me.

To the both of them, I said, Great! I wanted them to invite me over but Catherine declared it time to get me home. A reminder that my vulnerability did not change all structural foundation. Despite myself, my neck felt hot. I raised my shoulders and drew my chin to my neck in an effort to conceal it.

I said, You don't think I'll go home with you?

The wives were quiet and Katrina said, This is the second meeting.

I said I knew.

She said, These are your rules, Helen, not ours. I saw her look beyond me, knowing there were only dead, still trees, and realized she was communicating, just not with words.

I whimpered into my coat sleeve. They regarded me with concern and I noticed Katrina's eyes go glossy. I'm fine, I said. It's only the cold. But us three knew it was not. Rejection bit then, in general and with the two of them.

Catherine said, You sure you aren't free tomorrow? Or the night after? Catherine and Katrina let quiet sit and I imagined them stripping me in a white-and-beige living room, one piece of abstract art on the entire wall, terrible and unknowable, and the two of them measuring the important parts of my body: elbows, collarbone, smallest toes, distance from belly button to vulva. I thought, too, of my visit. My grandmother did not recognize the days of the week anymore, but I did. What is accountability if not honesty to those who don't know the difference. I said, No, I can't. I added I was sorry, though I could not quite bring myself to describe the nursing home, the drive, the baby clothes I had to pick up. I wanted to provide them with a crumb, enough to turn their bellies tight with hunger, and told them I had to go away for the weekend. *Away*, of course, meant the hours at the nursing home, and my hours in a cough syrup–induced sleep afterward. How else to manage an ache? The wives mmed.

6

IN THE FIRST FEW MONTHS I VISITED my grandmother, she cycled through a number of roommates. One transferred to another unit for more severe conditions; from what I surmised, she was a flight risk, as she kept getting out of bed and falling. Another died. I did not ask if my grandmother was in the room when it happened but I assumed it was so. Did the air change? Did she chill? Did she overhear last words only to be forgotten? Perhaps that would offer the dying woman a sense of relief in the end.

That day, the room was hers alone. My grandmother's state insurance did not cover the rate for a private room but the nursing home occasionally had intake gaps. A nurse aide had left the television on for her, and a rerun of *Cops* was blasting when I arrived. She said, Hello, and asked me to turn it off. I don't like to cause upset, she said, but I really hate that show.

It is a stressful one, I said.

Yes, she said. The good people look sad and scared, and the bad people look happy. I agreed. We talked about her doll. I brought a new outfit for it, as I made a habit of doing. At first, I brought the outfits only occasionally. Pink jumpsuits, sage rompers, camel coat with white T-shirt and black leggings, French-vanilla cardigan, reversible joggers, black and blue. The doll dressed better than I did. One visit, I appeared without an outfit, and she cried. I excused myself, humiliated and furious, and drove to the strip mall at the edge of town. I bought three outfits and returned.

With the room to ourselves, we changed the doll. My baby likes privacy, she said. I told her I understood. I removed the doll's dress, a red-and-white checkered number I'd found at a thrift store. I felt wasteful using the disposable wipes on a doll; I bought them for my patient, to keep by her bed, anything to help the underpaid nurse aides keep her clean and dignified, but I reasoned that even parents clean dolls for their children. I could not remember my parents doing such a thing but believed these were the details memory obscured because they were too poignant in affection.

Fold the dress, she said. Please. The dress was going into her hamper; housekeepers did patients' laundry once a week, for a small fee, which I paid, as it was not covered by insurance, but I folded it into neat thirds anyway. I thought of Katrina and the shirts and pants she arranged at the store. I tucked in the tag. I smoothed a wipe across each crevice of the doll. When I got to the face, she said, Careful, now, around her eyes. I patted the wipe on her bent and sparse lashes, then pressed her eyelids up and down. I kissed them, all stiff chemical.

You're sure these wipes are gentle enough for the baby? she said, and her eyes looked so alert in that moment, so clear and focused, bold even, ready to raise her voice if something was amiss. I said, Absolutely, I checked. I was not lying; the wipes were marketed for infants. I cleaned each toe, careful where nails would rest on a flesh baby. We even put socks on its feet. The doll was clean to the eye, especially the parts that would be concealed by the outfit.

To really let the disinfectant work, we should have let it dry out, but I could not resist her anxiety to hold the doll again, to make sure it was real, so I handed it back to her without hesitation. She kissed its face. She rested her cheek against the hairline of its bald head. I heard her say, I love you, over and over. I looked away, embarrassed at my envy.

After we dressed the doll in a red-and-green striped dress with black tights, for the holiday season, we looked out the double windows into the courtyard. Her room was on the ground floor. Her bed was closer to the door, so when she had a roommate, the windows were available based on their whims. Without a roommate, I pushed the divider all the way to the wall. I opened the blinds to the top.

I sat beside my grandmother and the doll and checked my phone. Wrong, I know, to not offer my full attention, but I was still getting used to the woman she had become—less aware, less coherent, less intelligible—and so I found myself skimming my camming app, getting a serotonin hit from messages. I noticed an increase in private notes using my name, which spooked me a little, though I reassured myself it was just the usuals who knew me: the librarian, the surgeon, or maybe even Amy's girlfriend, or Amy herself. Nothing about wanting to cut me up, only that they missed me, enjoyed me, hoped to see me come around again soon. I replied with kiss-ing emojis, red flesh unlike my own mouth, the retreating line of it. I liked that sort of confusing pursuit, the thrill and anx-iety of it. I recalled the fine blur of Catherine's nipples in her beach photo, and Katrina's, her wide areolas in full focus. I imagined them putting their breasts into my mouth and hav-ing me guess which nipple belonged to whom, a particularly fun game if their breasts were uneven. Photos did not relay quite so much detail, and I hoped the next time I saw them, they would let me touch them. Out of habit, I coughed into my elbow, then regretted it; I hated making my grandmother worry, and she fretted so often about her doll getting sick. Al-ways putting her ear to its chest to check for heavy breathing, peering up its nose for green snot.

Without looking at me, my grandmother said, Don't die, and then, I miss you, and I said, I miss you too. For the first time, I asked her if she missed my parents, my mom and my dad, as I referred to them with her. I said their first names too, wondering if it would help her remember them—and I hoped, increase her likelihood of saying she wanted them rotting somewhere—and with a full face, she told me she would give her eyes to see the small boy she still missed. Which small boy she might have been thinking of—her son or her grandson—I did not ask. In the most important ways, I knew they were both ghosts.

7

I BALANCED A BLUE BOWL OF YELLOW YEL-
low macaroni and cheese on my lap while I recorded a video of my feet. I arranged the phone
so it captured my toes and heels, then zoomed out two or
three frames; no need to feel claustrophobic while in the office. With room around the edges of what could be seen, I
proceeded to bend and stretch my toes against the floor,
watching my movements through the screen. I, like all who
innately doubt ourselves, have always appreciated a reliable
filter. I wondered when the wives would invite me out again, if
Catherine would ever actually tell me to come over for dinner.
I envisioned meal after meal, the three of us too nervous in
front of one another to eat, no one wanting to distend our bellies before sex. I considered writing messages on my stomach
and thighs the next time I sent them a round of photos, something coy to start—*professor do you give home visits* or *miss are
you available to check my gait*—and then direct: *Fuck me.* At my
desk, I answered two emails by directing the questioner to a
colleague. I felt peaceful.

Messages popped onto the screen during my live stream,

temporarily halting my ability to see my own video. How I appreciated those pauses. *Hey baby hi beautiful how old are you, anyway, sorry i missed you on monday, i always miss those perfect feet can we ever see your face hey hey are you really a dyke is it gel or shellac i love, love you honey.* I had one hour within receiving a message to send a reply, though I rarely did as a rule of thumb. I cracked the four small toes of my right foot against the floor, then the big one. The *pop!* release got a like or two most sessions.

Midway into my session, I received a private message request that read, *Don't freak out, it's only Katrina!!!* I dropped the spoon against my chest. I thought, How? I thought of the thousands of accounts like mine, the care I took to remain anonymous. Opening the message came with some risk; she would see that I had read it. I sat up and wiped the cheese sauce from my neck with the sleeve of my sweater. I watched the bubble signify Katrina was typing, stopping, typing, stopping, typing. Then: *Helen??*

I wrote, *send me your number,* and watched it appear. I felt powerful and cornered. I closed the app. I licked the remainder of the sauce from the bowl. I looked around; all heads ducked into cubes. I shoved my feet back into my boots, crossed the office without looking at any creature outside of the plastic fig plants, entered and departed the elevator alone, and called Katrina from the roof. The wind made me wish I'd brought my coat.

Katrina let the phone ring twice before saying, Helen! I heard a television in the background before it clicked off. It made me feel a little more equal to Katrina, knowing that she was not one of those people who preferred books to TV at all hours. For more reason than one, I bet Catherine wasn't home.

I said, Katrina. My eyes were open against the sharp air and watered on instinct. I told myself, No, you are not crying. No, you are not panicked. No, you are not afraid. You are resisting the urge to shut your body off in the face of the elements. I blinked and blinked as she spoke.

Not processing what she said at all, I said, Katrina, I am confused. I used the voice I performed when I participated in work meetings because my superior was out sick or on her three-month maternity leave. My words sounded measured, considered, not shrill, not panicked. Unnatural, too, and blatantly young in their desire to be read as mature.

Katrina said, What about? She added that she expected me to realize it was her sooner, and only included her name today because it didn't feel fun to be ignored.

I told her I didn't know how she found me. I could lose my job, I added, though that was a constant, vague fear, a perpetual imposter syndrome, and in fact, not my primary concern. I bent the toes of my boots against the concrete roof and pressed. My shins did not snap.

Katrina sounded surprised and sad. She said my name several times and told me she actually followed me already, she had just never messaged me. Once I told her the details, she figured it out.

I said, So why not mention it at the cafe? Or picnic? It was true I could only see followers if they made themselves public, or if they reached out directly. People could use any username they liked. Some people kept their messages all in one chain, so I could scroll up and see the interactions, but people could always close out and start a new chat. When a viewer started a new chat with me, I couldn't see our previous messages. The app required no formal registration, and as I asked for no payment, no real tracing. I felt paranoid she could see through my phone.

I'm sorry if I didn't go about this the right way, she said. I thought you'd find it cute.

I said, Cute? She said I sounded upset.

I repeated a line from an emotional regulation workbook I'd picked up shortly after both of my parents were incarcerated. The writers, a team of psychologists from a large university in the Midwest, suggested the word *upset* was camouflage for other feelings. When you say you are upset, the writers posited, are you angry? Are you lonely? Are you anxious? Are you afraid of being captured, caught, examined in unforgiving bright light? I told Katrina *upset* was a vague word. She did not reply, and I took care to listen for her breathing. To compare the sound of her breath to my mother's just then would have been too sharp, too taciturn even for me, and so I told myself I wanted to better remember her, certain she would soon become memory. Katrina chortled instead.

Catherine says stuff like that all the time, she said. Always pushing me on my word choice.

I said, Interesting.

I'm sorry this worked out this way, she said. I thought you'd find it funny.

I felt an emotion I might have labeled as upset, but in

truth, it was fear. To settle myself, I pressed my tongue out into the cold. I gagged. I asked if she would message me on the app from now on, instead. She said she might or might not and not to get my hopes up. I asked how Catherine felt about it: Did she use the app too? Did she proofread Katrina's messages? Ordinarily, the level of anonymity the app offered comforted me, but on that chilly roof, I felt vulnerable, uneasy. With a giggle, Katrina ignored my questions and told me the day and time to come to an address. She did not say *our house* or *the house* or *our place*, but the street name and numbers. I remembered Catherine's order to come to dinner when invited and wondered if I would taste their nipples, consider the weight of their breasts, or more. Before I spoke, Katrina hung up, and I coughed hard into the air. My spit blew back at me, sweeter than I expected.

From the roof, I watched gray snow on the state house, dimming its gold orb. I imagined my mother and father and Ryan perched at the top, not sliding down the curve but as stable as the birds. I waved, thinking of my family and of the wives; I wanted to see them, to learn the ways they would push me. I worried they might disappoint me, that there was no way they could match my instability. Too, I wanted a distraction from my father's request and from making the decision to help him toward freedom or not. I would see him soon and did not want to think ahead. I wanted incremental decisions: a dinner, a date, a message. I would take the little steps if someone else would run up behind me and push.

8

I BROUGHT A LOAF OF BLUEBERRY BREAD to the wives. I had never eaten such a thing, nor been aware of its existence, but on the evening of our first dinner, I stopped at a bakery a block from where they lived. Walking to their home, I told myself I was good, good, good, and convinced myself this was the perfect thank-you for the picnic I hadn't contributed to. I wondered if they would let me gargle their piss and felt the bread was a good opening.

I planned to circle the block once or twice before knocking on their door before texting, *Here!* Anticipation propelling me forward, that fine height of anxiety and desire. But Catherine and Katrina were waiting on their porch when I turned the corner. Both wore lemon-colored aprons tied at their necks and waists. They watched me approach, the loaf of bread in my hands, and I revisited the temptation to keep walking. When Katrina shouted, You came!, I stilled at the bottom of their steps.

It's a blueberry loaf, I said, and named the bakery. I wanted them to kiss me again. I wanted to slam my face into the top step of the porch. I wanted to split my front teeth. I wanted to know which would scream and which would call an ambulance. I wanted to know which would put her fingers in my blood and look at it straight on. I said, It's a lovely spot. Have you been?

Katrina waved me up the steps, ignoring my question, and opened the screen door. On the porch, an open recycling bin with two glass bottles arranged on stacks of newspaper. I was drawn in by the ornate caps and paused to read the labels—some sort of scotch. I wondered which one of them went for hard liquor and, briefly, whether or not all scotch actually came from Scotland. Catherine loves that bakery, Katrina said, and I felt her hand press the center of my spine. Rip it out, I was thinking. I imagined asking them to roast my vertebrae but I only stepped inside.

The wives held hands and walked before me. I was intimidated by a tall bookshelf to my left, as it was covered with knickknacks and framed photos. The living room and kitchen were separated by a door, a sign that the building was older than I had expected; nothing here was an open concept. Catherine opened the door and Katrina went to stir something on the stove. With Katrina's back to us, Catherine kissed me on the mouth and took the blueberry bread from my hands. I would have let her kiss or touch me anywhere, not out of a sense of love but a desire to see how far she would take things, how she might express herself, if she would watch for my reaction or if she would close her eyes and only listen to my squeaks and murmurs. She told me to come and I did; I looked over my shoulder and watched Katrina face the window, her shoulders open as though in anticipation of a great warmth.

Catherine wiped her hands on her apron and ushered me down the hall. The walls were deep blue. Above us, a light surrounded by a silver sconce. Did those come with the house? I asked. She did not look up and shook her head no. I hovered and she shooed me down down down the hall toward the closet at the foot of the stairs. I wanted to ask for Katrina, to call out to her, but when I opened my mouth, Catherine put her knuckles between my teeth.

Bite down, she said.

I thought, What? But I could not say a word, what with her hand obstructing my jaw, and so I bit down. Not even a bite, not really: pressure, pressure, pressure. I hoped she had doused her fist in bleach but I tasted only specks of flour trapped in lotion. She smiled and told me to step into the closet, then used her free hand to reach around me and open the narrow door. With her skin still in my teeth, I said, Oh. The word was only a throat rustle but that's all we needed.

In the closet, much was as I anticipated in the moments before we stepped inside; there were coats, rain jackets, sweatshirts with lined hoods. When she locked the door, I felt woozy. I gestured to my mouth and Catherine removed her fist just an inch. I rubbed my jaw, missing her presence that soon, and said, Did this door come with a lock? She told me she had it added. I thought, Oh shit. I put my palms out in front of me and grabbed. Maybe, I rationalized, there is a trick door. Maybe there is a hallway that leads to an escape route. Old houses hold mysteries, I thought. Of course, there were only fabrics concealing a wall.

Is that fur? I asked, and Catherine reached around me. In the dark, I could not see her face. The closet smelled of detergent.

We told you, Catherine said, voice small, no real furs, remember?

I'm only checking, I said. To make sure this is really your house. She requested to see my feet.

I said, Should we turn on a light? If she was going to end me, I wanted to see it coming, to allow my brain the relief.

No, she said, loving and impatient. I don't want a performance; I want to watch you as though you're alone.

She knelt before me but I understood I was the one under scrutiny. I did my usual poses: pointed, flexed, splayed, wiggled. With only the light that peered in the crack beneath the door, Catherine existed as an outline to me. Bent head and straight back.

I said her name over and over, unusual for me, as I had a lifelong embarrassment of my voice. And yet Catherine's focus demanded vocalization. I wondered if she wanted me to be loud enough that her wife might hear from beyond the door and masturbate to our actions.

Catherine's hands were warm when she removed my socks. I was apprehensive, of course, about the intimacy of being seen on someone else's terms. I explained how I set myself up on my bed, where I placed my feet against the wall. The window in my bedroom, I said. It does most of the work for me. When I breathed in, I felt certain I picked up the scent of my own wetness, and of garlic; I imagined Katrina eating roasted cloves down the hallway. Of course she knows about this, I thought. Of course, of course.

When Catherine was done with my feet, she stood and swayed. Jesus, she said, and I reached out both hands to steady her arms. Catherine grinned at me in the dark, full Cheshire, and I parted my lips in return. Catherine turned the light on and departed, closing the door politely behind her. She had left my socks folded beside me. I reached a hand into my underwear and rubbed myself, then left the closet, passed the front door—still unlocked, no barrier, nothing keeping me inside—and resumed my life, or at least a life, in the kitchen with the wives.

9

I SAT MYSELF DOWN. THE CHAIRS WERE wood. The table was a rectangle. In the center, a stout vase of purple pansies. Three white plates, the same from our picnic, sat on the table. One of the wives had arranged several spoons, forks, and knives beside each plate in a pattern I did not understand. Catherine placed a glass of water beside me and said Katrina was heating water for tea. I asked for something with caffeine, didn't matter what, and gave a small cough.

Catherine arranged three slices of bread on three smaller plates. Where does one find so many plates, I wondered. She cut into a slab of butter. Did you get a cold from the picnic? She said, Don't lie.

Really, it was way too cold, Katrina said. And you already had that cough at the cafe.

I closed my eyes and suckled Catherine's ChapStick off my lips and into my mouth. The coating tasted of plastic and comfort. I told them I did not have a cold, and I hoped they would read my denial as martyrdom, even though, as I reminded myself, I was not actually lying. I imagined how they might

tend to me if I developed a fever, a rash, an immobilizing in-
flammation. And then I realized, for the third or fourth time
that day, that my mother had not yet called. Girlish, again, I
left the ringer on.

Katrina put a large bowl of white rice cooked with saffron
and turmeric beside the flowers. On the other side, a spinach, potato, and cheese dish. Hunks of baked tofu sat in a sesame and brown sugar glaze. Catherine was generous enough
to identify the key components as my eyes passed over each
plate. When I thanked her, I believed she understood what
for. Tell us the kind of women you go for, she said.

Lesbians, I said. You know, and the bisexuals. They nodded, unimpressed. I told them about Emma. I pitched my
voice higher, though hers was all alto. When I go into the office, she's always like, *Hi, Helen, can I help you? Hi, can I get
you anything?* Always wanting to meet me for coffee because
she and her man live in my neighborhood.

Her man, the wives said, pretending to be scandalized.
Imagine such a thing, Catherine said.

You entertain her crush, Katrina said.

Only a little, I said. When she goes for coffee, I ask her to
get me some medicines. I paused, thinking of how smart I was,
having her sign for sleep aids that required an ID. Work is easy
for me, I continued, and I don't want to rock the boat. Plus,
the firm is trying to appeal to young people by letting us work
remotely as much as we want, so now I only go in, like, once
a month. I was exaggerating—really, I went in at least once a
week to keep up appearances—but I wanted to seem disinter-
ested, blasé about my income, as I imagined rich people were.

Katrina said, Does she seem happy to get you things?

I shrugged. I said, Well, she is an assistant.

That's cute, Katrina said. Catherine nodded and said they found me cute too.

We passed the bowls among the three of us, beginning with Katrina, going to Catherine, and then to myself. I took smaller portions than either of them, and each time, the wives told me to eat more. With the spinach dish, Katrina actually came around the table to spoon more onto my plate. Catherine was mixing her rice and spinach, a gesture that amused me in its childlike disregard for manners, and while I was watching Catherine with her spoon, Katrina kissed my mouth. There, she said after the kiss. She and I looked at the higher pile of food on my plate. She said, That's better, and went back to her seat.

I told them I adored their home. It smells like love, I said, embarrassed at my sincerity. I continued, That is, if you really live here, expecting them to laugh.

With a smile, Catherine said, We don't. She added a big piece of tofu to her plate, though she had not touched her rice concoction.

I laughed and rolled my eyes, eager to prove my ability to be in on the teasing. I said, What? You rented an Airbnb as a cover just for me?

They put down their silverware. They looked at each other for a long beat. I said, Guys? I looked at the table. I said, These are the same plates, aren't they? From the picnic. At their silence, I doubted my sense of reality. I wondered, not for the first time in my life but for the first time with the two of them, if I was forming lines between shifting dots.

Katrina asked me what I thought. Obvious, isn't it? Catherine turned her lips inside and I wondered if she was tasting her own bile. I thought, Slime is going to come out. I thought, No, blood. I thought, Is this how bodies break. Slowly and neatly. Katrina turned redder and redder; her tawny complexion morphed as though her head had been inside the oven. They opened their mouths, Catherine first, Katrina immediately after, and no liquids spewed. Oh, I realized. They had only been trying not to laugh at me. I laughed too and was surprised none of my organs flushed out. Perhaps my esophagus was too narrow for all that.

I said, Come on. I placed my fork on the tablecloth and picked up my butter knife. Only Catherine had a cutting knife. I said, Tell me if you're serious or I'm going to leave.

They looked at each other worriedly and laughed. Together, they said, Helen! Together, they were on their feet at my side again. Katrina crouched herself on the floor so her head was level with my chest and Catherine stood behind me. She put her hands on top of my head.

I'm sorry, Katrina said. We tease so much, we forget it's confusing when people don't know us well.

Catherine massaged her fingertips into my scalp. I wondered if she noticed I'd washed my hair for them. My conditioner smelled of vanilla, but I did not think it matched the scents in that kitchen. We're normal, she said. As normal as you.

I said, This is your home. I felt relieved that I had perhaps found them—women wild enough to consume the air around us in the way I wanted to be drained. This crazy was both what I desired and feared.

They said, Yes!

Catherine kept her hands on my head, and I turned to Katrina, who wore an expression I recognized, one of muted anxiety and thrill. She had looked at me this way when we three were at the reservoir, an even earlier us. I thought of the hunks of bread, the thick layers of sweet. How my mouth worked around it all, the expansion of my jaw. The joint ached the next day but from stress or force I could not tell. Perhaps they were one and the same.

I said, Where did you buy this table?

They said, Pier 1. Katrina said they found it on sale and Catherine demurred with the quiet embarrassment of the up-per class. Katrina and I were alike in that way, eager to boast about deals we'd discovered in an effort to prove our smarts and worthiness. Catherine, I believed, would sort items from the highest to lowest price online, if not for Katrina's enthusi-asm at finding such a steal.

I said, The living room.

Catherine said, What about it? She nodded toward the room as though I had not walked through it myself.

I said, There are framed photos. They waited. I said, Show me yourselves. I pushed back my chair—a low noise startled me, only a scrape, but I uttered a small Sorry—and stood at full height. I led the wives—or at least, that is what I told myself.

Any family could have lived in that room, filling the shelves with bought or borrowed books that eventually overflowed to the short glass coffee table. Porcelain ballerinas and clowns, cartoonish and threatening in their amplified emotions, must have been gifts from doting great-aunts. Three living succulents—I touched them, to check for falsity and perpetual longevity—were equally spaced in front of a thick copy of Elizabeth Bishop's collected works. My family could not have lived in that room; I could not have lived in that room.

I closed my eyes. I put my hands on the bookshelf and steadied myself. My head felt light, wicked. I laughed. I heard movement behind me, quiet, considered. With my eyes closed, I passed my hands over the picture frames. Tall, short. Glass, wood. I lifted a heavy one and turned. I said, Tell me all about her. I looked at the photo only briefly. Just a woman who, unlike myself, had been lucky enough to get the braces she needed as a child. She was smiling smiling with her eyes shut: easy, happy, closer to unafraid than not.

The wives leaned forward. They held hands. Katrina was still chewing something when Catherine said, You chose a difficult photo. They exchanged a look and I understood them as liars, smart, but not smart enough, and still I did not hit or kick or crawl between their legs.

I said, Tell me everything. I moved the frame behind my back. Neither tried to take it.

She's an ex, Catherine said. I asked if it was her ex-wife, wondering if the three of them had an arrangement, and together, they shook their heads no, Katrina looking offended, and Catherine, ruffled. We met her from the app,

Catherine said, and chewed her lips before looking to Katrina for assistance.

I said, Tell me more. Understand I felt more powerful than I had in months, maybe in years. I was getting what I wanted, seeing them scramble, watching them try to prove themselves to me.

Catherine said there were no hard feelings; throuples don't work for everyone. I watched Katrina; her face revealed the vulnerability of her thinking. I looked at the photograph again. The ex was short and blond and happy. I thought, Like Catherine. I thought, Is not every woman a transient glint. I thought, Jesus.

We have loads of wedding photos, Katrina said. I don't know if that feels, you know, weird for you to see or not, but we have them all over the place. She passed me a heavy silver frame. Their faces, beaming at each other, filled my focus. Behind them, leaves in full fall. Above them, warm light. With a squint, I noticed Katrina wore fake lashes, and Catherine, bronzer. I said I needed to sit and I lowered myself to the floor.

Why keep the photo, I said, if it's over? The wives looked at each other and told me they'd keep one of me too, and it was then I resolved to remain in their lives as more than a stilled life, more than the subject of a future woman's insecurities. When else would I meet crazier women, I rationalized. I told them, Cool.

Katrina returned with her arms behind her back. Once we made eye contact she put her hands in front of her with a big flourish: empty. Catherine laughed from her belly. I told them I didn't understand and hoped they understood how happy my confusion made me, how deeply aroused I felt at this instability. Can't you see? Katrina said. You have us. As she spoke, she smirked in the direction of her wife.

We're so good to you, Catherine said. You don't need paperwork.

We could forge it, Katrina said. She sat beside her wife and kissed her before telling me they could add my name if it made me feel better.

I'll bet your signature is like a child's, Catherine said when they paused, and I kissed her on the mouth.

We three kissed one another for what felt like a long while. My legs went numb. They did a lot of checking in and I said a lot of, Yes, I'm good, and you? What about you? Katrina tired first and told us to keep going, she was happy to watch, and Catherine and I kissed for a while longer. I considered asking if either wife wanted to sit on my face, but I feared rejection too much to speak. Then Katrina put her cheek to my clavicle, ignoring my breasts altogether, and said she'd been thinking of her mother a lot lately, missing her, and wanted to visit her up north soon. It seemed like a previous thread of conversation, and I expected Catherine to answer in some way. Catherine looked up at me through her lashes; her hair was blond enough that her eyelashes were white, at least at that angle, in that light, and I said, You should go up some weekend, no?

Katrina inched closer. The three of us were already touching, bodies lined up on the carpet, and with Katrina's movement, her arm rested on mine fully, so I could feel the weight of her lean frame. I looked at the ceiling. She said, You know, what really inspired me is that weekend you had away.

I said, Me? I thought of my visit to the nursing home. I thought, Oh, fuck.

Katrina said, Yes. It got me thinking about how important it is to prioritize people we don't see every day. I can't stand thinking of my mom alone . . . Living in the house she raised this whole family in, you know? The world passes by outside and she just talks to people on the phone. She said, My mother is practically living in a cell, and there's nothing I can do. But I can visit at least. Right?

I imagined my mother's face in the living room window, observing the three of us as a scientist might. She would write terrible notes but relay the key truth: sick, sick, and sicker. I wanted to walk into the kitchen, push my face into the warm rice, and howl.

Instead, I said, I can tell you love her. I hesitated, then kissed her hairline. Her skin tasted chemical, like foundation. I squinted and saw she'd applied it unevenly, and clumps of her freckles beamed out from beneath lighter layers. I told her they should take the trip. Catherine tapped my ear and said, The semester is really bogging down on me. Maybe, someday soon, you could take her?

I said, To Maine?

She said, It's southern Maine. A few hours each way. You can do the drive in a day, but it's less tiring to sleep a night there.

I felt challenged, caught. I said, Wouldn't we be happier if the three of us went together? I said the right thing, understand, because they both kissed me again. Catherine asked if I wanted water, and I said not really, as I did not want her to leave. But still, she untangled herself from us and returned with two glasses: one filled with only ice, the other with water, for Katrina. I thought, How strange, chewing ice. I worried, foolishly, about Catherine's molars. Then she told me to remove my underwear and stand on the couch. Eyes open, she said. I wondered if she would take a fork or her finger to my pupils and drag them out. I hoped so.

10

I SAID, SERIOUSLY? BUT I KNEW SHE WAS serious and wanted her to be. What was intimacy if not a space to command and to listen. I imagined Catherine pouring cold water over my head and massaging my scalp. Maybe she'd put a cloth over my face and pour from my forehead down. When the wives did not answer, only smiled, I told them I wasn't ready to be filmed and they nodded. Of course, they said, as though we were negotiating the start time of a meeting. I suppose, in a way, we were.

The couch felt like leather and I told them as much. I was sweating and worried my feet would leave slicks in my place. I was embarrassed at my early arousal, my dry throat, and my nausea. I wondered if the wives would clean my vomit from the cushions but I swallowed down my heat. The couch is actually vegan, Katrina informed me from her spot on the rug. We had to special order it but it's great because shit just wipes right off.

I said, Literally? Feeling their eyes on my back, I unzipped my jeans and pulled them to my ankles, my underwear looped beneath my thumb. I squatted to tug them off; there is no elegant way to do this, and I hoped they looked away, but when I glanced over my shoulder, I saw two pairs of amused eyes. I gave a wink, still in a crouch, and when they did not laugh nor chuckle nor even flinch, I felt happier and more seen. I stood back up like a rod.

Not literally, Catherine said. Or at least, I don't think. We don't play like that.

I nodded toward the wall. What about piss? I said.

That's probably fine, Katrina said. When I squirt, it's not an issue. Catherine murmured her assent. I felt comfortable then, listening and imagining, my legs gaining goosebumps and my nipples erect beneath my sweater and bra.

I heard a glass rattle. I said, Did you want me to get you more water? I thought I would earn a point for my attentiveness.

Catherine said, No. She said, Stand straighter. I did. She said, Turn your legs out.

I opened my hips and pointed my feet to the sides. I used the wall to steady myself. I said, Like this?

Katrina said, No! Your knees are bent.

I said, What? The fastidiousness delighted me. I stood on my tiptoes, unsteady.

Katrina pushed my pelvis forward and grabbed my thighs one at a time. She tugged at my knees and calves. My hips resisted and she pushed and pushed. She did not touch my vulva and I wondered how long I would remain in this contortion. I apologized for my lack of flexibility and Katrina said I would improve with time. Then I felt the ice against my perineum.

I thought, Oh! I thought, Oh. I widened my legs. The wives asked for my safe word and I said, Confinement.

Katrina sat beside my feet as Catherine manipulated the ice cube. You seem very warm, Catherine said, and Katrina added that my face and chest were more than a little red. I wondered when they'd devised this plan. Had they been intending this all night, worried that I might exit their home without having let them ice my skin? When Catherine pressed the wet cube to my vulva, I gasped. I said, Thank you.

Sounding happier than I'd yet heard her—giddy even— she said, You're welcome. Catherine rubbed the cube in the crease between my vulva and my thighs, up and around and across my mound, and tapped it across my clitoral hood. My hood is long and thick even when aroused, so it was not until she turned the cube to a chiseled edge and pressed it between my labia that I really shuddered. After a few minutes, I felt the fingers of her other hand reach around and tug up my hood to reveal my clitoris. I braced myself, expecting direct, wet cold, but she only flicked it with her pointer finger. When I jumped in place, knees knocking inward, she passed the cube to Katrina, who stood beside me and placed it in my mouth. She did not have to ask, as my mouth was already a happy, open circle.

Hours later, at the door, Katrina asked me to tell them one thing.

I said, Why just one? I had my coat on but it was unbuttoned. My body felt larger from all their focused touching. I shifted between my feet and welcomed the familiar soreness of my upper thighs against my vulva. I felt satiated, and desired to touch the wives, to return the bliss, lest they rely only on each other and freeze me out. I imagined leaving matching mouth bruises on their lower bellies. I wanted them to ask me to stay the night, but Catherine showed no signs of it. Instead, in the kitchen, she loaded up several containers of Tupperware with rice and spinach and chickpeas. She placed a paper into the bag, perhaps a love note or a receipt for my share of the ingredients. In the doorway, I wanted to push past them and find, for the first time, their bedroom.

If I ask you for too much, we'll get nowhere, she said. Catherine rested her face on Katrina's shoulder and smiled at me, sleepy. I wondered if that was how she looked in the mornings: easy, unalert. I wanted to ask what they would do after watching me walk along the street and around the corner. Would they eat rice in bed, go down on each other, and talk about me? They held hands, which convinced me I was right.

I said, What's the one thing? I thought perhaps if I answered correctly, they'd invite me to stay.

We have a little bet going on between us, Catherine said. It doesn't matter, but we disagree.

So we're hoping you can settle it, Katrina continued. They looked impish then, my wives.

I said, How do you know I won't choose the middle to please you both?

Katrina pushed several strands of hair behind Catherine's ear and repeated the gesture on herself. That's the thing with this question, she said. There's, like, no gray area. It's just an answer.

Catherine said, Are you an only child?

I said, What?

She repeated it and Katrina said, You know, do you have brothers or sisters or not? Or half-siblings, whatever you want to call them. When I didn't answer, she said, Catherine has you pegged as an only child, but I thought you have a lot of big-sister energy. Who is right?

I said, I have no siblings, kissed them both, and left. Shaken by their perceptiveness, I walked down the steps and onto the street and did not turn to wave or see their faces. Our strange intimacy spooked me, not because of the sex or the suddenness but because of the easy familiarity of the thrill the wives brought me. I thought, Go further, and then they did. I thought, Go crazier, and they did. With the wives, the chaos offered a controlled bliss. Oh, to have thought I understood.

11

ENTERING PRISON ISN'T LIKE THE MOV-
ies. Maybe it is; I don't remember anything I
experience on a screen. I hadn't told my father
that I was coming; I didn't want to give him extra time to
scheme, to decide which memories to keep for himself. No
couples had sensed the little ghost before, and I felt newly empowered to revive my brother. When I signed in at the front
desk, I was lucky to discover my father hadn't removed me
from his visitor's list after our last phone call.

The visitor's room was all cream walls and plastic folding
tables and chairs. We sat where we were directed, just as we
had the last time I had visited, two or three months prior,
when I had told him I would not return if he kept pressing
about the statement. Together, we told the guard, Thank you.

My father thumbed the circles under his eyes. His fatigue,
like mine, grows purple. Mauve in the noon light. I had him
surprised, eager, optimistic. He was as pleasant as any man
who thought he was about to win. The windows were too high
to get much of a view, but we caught sight of snow-covered
pitch pines well enough. Can almost taste the icicles, my

dad said, nodding with his head and not his hands. During visits, it's especially important for him not to make sudden movements.

So beautiful, I said. I described the drive and comforted my father when he tensed up about street conditions; he had an ongoing fixation with black ice leading to my death. It started when I was a kid and split my top lip on the board-walk. Angry ocean water had reared up and covered the cement, my dad explained to me when I was all of eight years old and an unhappy mess. Anger leaves a lot we can't see until we drop from life.

When I grazed my fingers against my jeans, I wanted to ask my father how his jumpsuit felt. Did such things wear to softness or did the scratch rub and rub and rub. Instead, we talked about the desserts.

The vending machine had a surprising amount of variety. I have never asked, but I can only assume the vendor who fills the black box wants to birth joy when he can. The machine does not take credit cards so I use dollar bills and select our treasures: apple pie peach pie lemon pie blueberry pie raspberry pie chocolate cream pie mango key lime pie vanilla pudding pie. The friendlier guard teased me as I carried my bounty, arms wrapped to my chest as if the pies would spoil if I dropped them, as though the plastic would not protect what is manufactured to delight. When I smiled at the guard, bashful and irritated, I wondered if he ever beat my father.

We ate these when I was a kid, my dad said, 'cept they came in brown paper wrappers.

Same brand? I said. I imagined my grandmother choosing

pies and carrying them home in a knitted sack. She would have cradled them. No, resented. She would have split them in two and watched her little boy's joy. She would have eaten with all her teeth.

Yeah, yeah, he said. Same brand. My mom used to heat them up for me when I got home from school. When he looked to the ceiling, I imagined hot hot hot fruit filling leaking from both our eyes.

That's very sweet, I said. I'd heard stories of my father as a boy: an oddity as an only child in his generation, and small for his age, slim through the shoulders and the face. An easy target. I wondered if he and I were the same in that way, if we'd inherited not empathy through survival but bitterness. Across from him, I dug into the vanilla pudding pie and wondered if he resented my ability to leave.

He took the peach and said, You ready to hear it? I could not remember if this is how he told me my brother was dead; I thought not. I reminded myself I had been a good girl for so many years; I wanted my parents to love me, or at least like me, and so I didn't pry about the ghost in our home

I said, No. We shuffled paper napkins between us. I said, Yes. I said, Can you tell me about Ryan? Sugar and sweat filled my nostrils, a simple comfort against panic. I reminded myself I had a fresh bottle of cough syrup waiting for me in the rental car. Purple purple purple: bliss.

He said, You've been visiting my mom?

I told him yes. He asked if she was fine and I said she did not seem abused or hurt or frightened. I mentioned the doll and the TV and her lunches.

He perked up. She likes the food all right?

Yeah, I said. She eats the food. I described the puddings, pistachio and chocolate, the vegetable stews, and the rolls. I told him she offered to share her lunches and he sounded proud. I asked him to tell me something about Ryan and he looked to the window.

I said, Dad. I predicted my father would not give me what I wanted, would not entertain my happiness, would not open a scab and allow me to suckle blood. I imagined leaning forward just enough to attract an *ahem* from the guard by the door, and telling my father that if he did not give me a nice story, a family memory, a glimmer of the dead person I thought about every day, I would scream. The guards would come to our sides, and I would be vague, just a hysterical woman, just the usual fare in the visiting room of a men's state corrections facility. I would ruin my father's small joys to show him I was not so meek anymore, that I could and would gnaw back. Instead, I stayed back in my chair, posture poor, as always, and said, Dad?

He told me he was thinking. He said he thought Ryan's favorite color might have been purple, and dropped his wrist and wiggled his fingers, making a face. I knew my father was trying to appear effeminate, trying to mock gay men, and because I wanted him to go deeper, to tell me more, I laughed from my chest. He laughed too, showing off his gums and graying teeth, and I remembered he, not my mother, taught Ryan and me to floss after every meal. Cheaper than cavities, he told us, as though we had ever been to a dentist.

I think you're right about purple, I said, though only to

humor him. I asked him to tell me his favorite thing about Ryan, surprised at the honesty of my request.

Without hesitation my father told me Ryan was easy to love. I said, What? He told me Ryan had that way about him: simple, accepting, soft. Didn't put up fights, didn't make people beg or plead or reason with him. He was good, easy. I asked if Ryan always took his medicine or if he hit, as I did when my parents wrestled antibiotics into my cheeks.

My dad stretched his arms out and cracked his elbows. I think he just swallowed his pills, he said. I don't remember no fights. He asked me if I remembered anything and I said no, nothing like that. I wondered what sort of bond Ryan and I would have developed as adults, what camaraderie we might have built as the gay children of adults who didn't know what to do with us. If Ryan would pursue couples, two men eager to care for him and to hurt him, and if he would be good for them, easy. Punctual, reliable, a good cook and good in bed. Not as exciting as me, not as vibrational, that would be our joke between us. I asked my father to tell me something else and he only reminded me our time was close to done and mentioned his court-appointed attorney. How he thought I might have been satisfied I still do not understand.

He told me then his friends wouldn't respect him if they ever found out what he was doing. I said, What? He told me he wasn't used to giving up his side of things so early. But you wouldn't screw over your old man, he said. Would you.

I'm your daughter, I said.

He said, And?

I wouldn't screw you over, I said, though I was thinking

about doing precisely that. I tensed my fingers against the remaining lemon curd but did not squeeze; he loved it so.

Given that you're my kid, he said, your statement could be a big help to actually get parole.

I said to my father, I know what happened to Grandma, Dad. I don't want to upset you, but you know I know. His face stayed set and I understood all that was beneath it: fear, fear, fear, fear, fear. Terror that I would act as selfishly as he had. That I would only make low-level promises. That I would think of him, worry about the conditions he lived in, fret if he was clean or frequently fed. And then I would forget, grow lazy, complacent, center myself, repress until the shame set in, leave him in there to wait and rot and think, surrounded by bodies that register him only as flesh in the doorway, and all he'd have would be the worst of himself, his animal thoughts, all that he could not escape.

I said, What is it you want me to say in the letter? Sitting across from him, I was scared of his anger and of how evil I could be, how much like him, how cold.

Just that you love me, he said. And you believe in me, and how hard I've been working, and well, you know, that you've been doing your visits, and you know my mom is doing so much better, so it's not like . . . He trailed off and we both heard the omission: It's not like she actually died. It's not like I killed her.

I asked him when his attorney wanted the letter by. This question shames me in its cruelty; I was never planning to write it. Inside jails, my parents were the most reliable they'd ever been, and the kindest. Understand I was still such a small girl.

My father motioned to smack me on the forearm, as he'd done since I was small, and caught himself. A guard snapped at him anyway and my father ducked his head. I pushed the pastries toward him, told him to eat up. He devoured, sweet pastries worked into his mouth, and when we hugged good-bye, our arms barely grazing, my chest bumping into his lean stomach, I watched flakes stay tight to his lips and admired their refusal to be forgotten.

I told him to tell his attorney I'd come to his office on Saturday and go over the statement. I promised him I would type it up and everything, an assurance that always impressed my parents, as neither ever learned how to use a computer. I told him I was happy, happy, happy to do it. I do not remember my father's expression but I know I looked at him nowhere but in his eyes.

12

I STOPPED INTO A CUMBERLAND FARMS not far from my apartment to purchase another box of Nyquil. This location ran low on the syrup (I assumed because people gave it to their children to make them sleep on car rides and weekend mornings) and so I emotionally prepared myself for the disappointment of resorting to the gel tablets. The cashier, as ever, insisted on recording the information from my license, as though he did not know it by heart. In addition to off-brand boxes, I bought three Little Debbie chocolate cakes, and nail clippers. Feeling disgusted with myself, ashamed of my dirtiness, I clipped my nails in the car. I was ovulating and my skin spurned grease. I pressed my forehead to the wheel and when a group of teenage boys hollered for my attention, I admit, I jumped. Grease shone in my wake. Even in the fluorescent parking lot, even locked in, I felt unsafe. I swallowed two tablets with spit.

I thought there might be barriers. Other people inside or, worse, at the door. I did not know how to explain myself. I should have thought about the consequences of showing up not only unannounced but in that sort of wired, unhappy state. But messages on the app reminded me how badly I was missed, and though I was not sure which wife—or both—was sending them, I did not want to lose out on our game, did not want to ask for clarity, to seem too high-maintenance, too needy to hang. I was also desperate for a distraction from my father, and thought if these women let me into their home—or if they didn't, and we fought on the porch, or if they told me to go away, to stop being such an invasive species—I would have a fresh disaster to nurse, a new reason to hate myself aside from the obvious ones.

Katrina surprised me by opening the door before I knocked. I assumed Catherine assigned herself that role: opening the door to unexpected knocks, answering unknown numbers, chatting with people who said, Are you the MacArthurs? But that evening, it was Katrina who greeted me, saying my name, then calling me sweetheart.

I heard Catherine yell from inside, Get in, get in! It's frigid, she said. I struggled with my shoes, mostly because I did not want to drop the three Little Debbies flattened in one hand. Katrina stooped and went for my laces. I tightened my leg, braced my ankle for stillness. My cold toes tried to make themselves smaller and could not.

Easy, she said. Just let me do it!

I said, You don't have to do that. I felt embarrassed, wild. Would I have let me in? No, I would not be this kind, this easy. If anyone approached my door, I would dread the reveal of my slum, my panic. I would retreat to my bathroom, hoping they could not hear my footsteps. To Katrina, I said, Thank you.

Katrina removed my shoes. There was already space for me beside their snow boots and house slippers and the sight made me release a low noise, a howl of a sort, or a whimper. She kissed my feet through my damp socks. From sweat or snow I did not know. I curled my arch for her and she put her forehead to my toes. She said, Yes. She led me to the kitchen and I said, Yes.

Two bowls of pasta sat half-eaten on the table. Catherine was shredding a block of Parmesan into a third. She said, Honey. She said, Sit! She pointed her foot at the chair I'd sat in before and I obeyed, surprised and gleeful when she told me I was looking under the weather. How I longed to be perceived as weak. Katrina draped a blanket around my shoulders, which Catherine noted as smart before asking if I needed the heat turned up. Before I could answer, Katrina said she would do that now, what a good idea. I put my chocolate cakes on the table beside the amaryllis.

Catherine placed a bowl of fusilli with chickpeas and parsley in oil with red pepper flakes in front of me. Everything glistened under the good, artificial light in their kitchen. I said it smelled divine. Catherine squatted behind my chair and put her hands around my shoulders. She told me to eat. Adrenaline moved my jaw; I wanted to savor but I could not, my body beyond me. I let the oil onto my lips and chin. I looked to Katrina; her pimples had healed. I licked my oil.

I said, Did you use a lot of heavy cream? I wanted to tell them about my father's request and my agreement. I wanted them to tell me not to worry about it. He made his own choices, didn't he? I wanted to see them shake their heads at my parents' mistakes. I wanted to hear them tell me I was good even if I didn't help him. That if I refused to help him, I would be even better. I wanted permission for fearing my worst fear: that he, that my mother, would become free with or without me, and I'd go back to lonely girlhood, no longer useful, no longer a lifeline.

Instead, Catherine explained the dish was vegan, except for the Parmesan at the end. They blended cashews in water to develop a rich cream. I can show you sometime, she said, if you like. I lied and said I would. I wiped the snot from my upper lip before I realized I had been crying. I emptied my plate and she scooped more onto it.

I said, I'm sorry I didn't call. I claimed it wasn't like me, though of course, it was. I flashed to Emma surprising me in the bathroom and wondered if she was the type to show up without warning. No, I saw her as the sort of woman who was always stimulated, always connected, always on the phone or typing or emailing or liking. If it weren't for that man of hers, I told myself, she would open her home to me at any time. What she would do better than the wives I couldn't imagine—drifting from my present was not a response to their failures to care but rather a sign of my distrust of accepting anything offered at my feet. Always another woman, always another home.

Katrina paused in tearing her garlic roll. From across the table, I watched fat glow on her fingers. She waved my apology away, then put a piece of bread into her mouth. Her jaw moved in tight circles and I imagined clinging to her molars. I felt dizzy, woozy, foolish. Katrina asked if I was sick and I denied it.

I imagined, as I had during most meals since my parents went to jail, what my mother and father ate. My father told me it was all good, all good, nothing fancy but fine, and of course, my mother said nothing. I did some research during conference calls at work; nutrition value was low, fresh produce negligible. Not fit for dogs, a journalist wrote. I agreed. To the wives, thinking of my father and his thawed corn and soft meat, I said, I need to tell you something.

Catherine said, Do you?

Her question was enough to deter me. I said I wasn't sure. She said, Eat, and when I shook my head at more food, Catherine asked if I wanted tea, lemon or peppermint, to help me digest. We have it every night, she said. I did not answer and Katrina put a mug before me.

Sniff first, Catherine said. Tell us what you think. I did exactly that: I smelled the steam and guessed mint. The wives shook their heads and I said lemon and they shook their heads and, feeling ridiculous, I said key lime raspberry chocolate mango Scottish breakfast jasmine green grape. I don't think a grape tea exists, Catherine said, and they were both smiling.

May I drink? I said, and they said yes. I swallowed twice and felt a deep burn in my body. I was wondering if it was poisoned, or even just drugged with a narcotic or two. I wanted to be a good girl, complacent, and wondered if they'd put me in pajamas or rest me on their roof for the night. I finished the mug.

What was it? I said. Cyanide? The wives laughed and Catherine said I was so small, such a smart girl; Katrina said they'd been testing me to see if I had that gene, the special one that lets you smell cyanide as almonds. But bitter, I continued, thinking out loud, hoping a factoid I'd picked up from listening to crime TV while visiting my grandmother was accurate. The wives laughed and laughed. I was hoping I would die, sure, but I had more to experience with these women, more rolls toward death—death couldn't happen so soon. Katrina was still laughing when she walked across the room.

Catherine told me to hold on. I did hold on, if you can believe it. I held my fork in the air and kept my mouth a little open. I felt loved and special, obedient, a winner. I was doing all the right things. Then Katrina returned from the fridge with an unmarked bottle filled with a dark purple liquid.

I asked what the glass contained, hoping it was in fact a fatal drug, and Katrina explained it was a homemade elderberry syrup. Easy, she said. You boil the flowers of the berries with a lot of sugar and honey. She added, Never the seeds.

And keep it in the fridge, her wife said. Otherwise it'll get mold. She had already removed the cap.

Oh, I said. I wanted more tests, to play sick as long as I needed. Too, I wanted their effort after effort to heal me, their little damsel. I said, I don't mess with natural remedies.

Your mouth tastes like cough syrup, Catherine said. It's ugly. And terrible for you.

That's not true, I said, though it was, of course. I nodded toward the bottle and said, That might make someone sick.

Nothing makes you sick, Katrina said. Remember, you said it yourself at the restaurant. You're a tank. She put air quotes around *tank* and I reddened. I thought, yes yes yes yes finally yes.

Nothing makes you sick, Catherine said and nodded to-ward Katrina. You are sick. And anyway, only the entire bottle hurt you. I shook my head no and she motioned to Katrina, who came around behind my back. I resisted less than I might have expected. Katrina got a hold of my jaw and I spilled my mouth. I imagined spitting in Catherine's lovely face but what rationale did I have? I reasoned she was only loving me. Then Katrina asked me to show them my blood.

13

THE BEDROOM WAS MOSTLY BED. THE comforter was lilac. I asked again if they minded that I was on my period—one never knew who paled in the face of fresh red—and the wives said they had towels for precisely these circumstances. The mattress spanned much of the far wall and stretched into the center of the room. Tables and shelves with books and makeup were shoved into the room's crevices and gaps. Beneath one window, a record player. They sat on the bed. My breasts felt weighted in arousal and I wondered if they had noticed my nipples through my shirt, or if these were the sort of women who were above looking. I wanted them to demonstrate their noises and faces at all stages of arousal and climax, so I could be more present in the moment should I manage to please them. There, I could think, I did it! To the couple, I said, Wow.

Catherine asked me to describe the room of the last woman I had been with and I said, Um. Katrina nodded to me and shifted her hips along the bed. I said the woman had come over to my place, and I described my bedroom honestly: ratty, dusty, altogether embarrassing for an employed woman in her thirties. I added that the woman did not stay long enough to admire my good morning light and the wives appeared pleased, though it of course occurred to me that they had not yet been inside my home, much less around ten in the morning.

Katrina put her hand down the front of her underwear and said, You're sure this woman's name isn't Emma? I paused, surprised and unsure of the woman's name; I told them I thought it was Kayley or Cara. Catherine asked if I thought about Emma and I told her not really. She looked at me as though she knew the answers to all of her own questions, as if she had been watching me for a very long time, and I sat with my desire to lower myself to their wood floor and ask for forgiveness. I felt then that these women knew too much. That I was so foolish to believe in my own autonomy. Catherine asked why I didn't go to Emma's place instead of theirs, as though she had been hearing my thoughts.

I considered my response seriously and ran down my own list of rationales: Emma and I were not close in a real way, and besides, she had that boyfriend living with her. I could have perhaps enticed her for a drink and made out with her a little but it would not be all this.

I left feeling exposed, I told the wives. After the last time, with the ice and the questions. They nodded because of course they remembered. I told them I wanted to see if they would repeat their behavior, if they would introduce another barrier to establish a simple dominance, or if they would let me come closer, if they would allow themselves to be seen or touched. I wanted to know if I would forever be an object for them to examine via sight and experiment. Catherine gestured for me to come between them and pulled Katrina's hand onto her stomach. They laid before me like parallel questions.

Our three bellies were swollen. I rubbed both wives through their underwear. Catherine looked focused, content, not relinquishing any control but allowing me to perform. Katrina roiled. I went down on her for a while, rubbing Catherine intermittently, though I was distracted, I admit. I kept thinking of Emma, imagining what her labia might look like: uneven, I guessed, longer on the right and shorter on the left. I wanted to inform both of them that this distraction was their own fault; Emma hadn't been in my mind, and rarely was, until their curious interest in her existence. My bloated stomach provided a nice cushion against the mattress and I continued going down on Katrina and thinking about Catherine's jealousy. At first I delighted in the notion of Catherine—refined, well-bred Catherine with her books and her manners and her delicate palate—only inches from obsession over little Emma. I liked imagining her just moments from hurting those she loved in an effort to keep them close. And, too, I worried Catherine's jealousy would decrease my attraction to her, that her meanness would fade into a bitterness, that it would be all Emma Emma Emma and Emma would be only a blip in my life but a boulder in the wives' anxiety.

Their comforter was still on the bed—we hadn't pulled the blankets down or rearranged the sheet, and I wondered if I was making a mess through my own underwear. Catherine closed her legs and let my hand stay enclosed between her thighs. When she moved behind me to remove my underwear,

I shifted up to my knees. The movement caused me to lift my mouth from Katrina and she exhaled, then laughed. Catherine and I laughed too. I noticed Catherine had folded my underwear and placed it beside me, where she sat before, and when she put her mouth on me, she shifted my hips and legs and steadied. I returned to Katrina. I came very quickly, long before Katrina did, and I closed my eyes with my face against her. She laughed again and said it was all right, she was on a medication, that's why she took so long. Catherine, who had been rubbing my feet, smacked my clitoris with a finger. I shuddered and returned to Katrina, who did take a long time, I'll admit, and who did orgasm after she directed my fingers inside of her and she rubbed her own clitoris. Catherine, who continued massaging my feet and calves off and on during this, her hands steady, solid, even eager, sat upright behind me. Katrina and I faced her in time to watch her orgasm, slow, grinding against the heel of her palm. When she was done, she said it was the second; we'd missed the earlier one. She said, I'm always first, and looked right at me.

None of us had brushed our teeth or washed our hands. I wondered if Catherine had dislodged any blood from my menstrual cup but she distracted me from my hypothesizing, saying, It's so funny we made it to the bedroom and didn't use any of this. She pulled a box out from the top drawer of their bedside table. Katrina opened it and gestured like she was the model on a game show.

I admired the toys and tools and said, Wow.

Catherine said, Next time? And because it was so clearly a question, so clearly a vulnerability, and also, because I wanted it so certainly, and I wanted to give in to my want so deeply, I said, Of course.

Katrina said, Did you get what you were looking for? Be honest.

My instinct was to tell myself I had no idea what I was looking for from moment to moment. The wind could change my sense of self, as could poor natural light, or a stomach upset from food left on the counter a day too long. And I recognized then that the vulnerability I sought from them, the ability to see and touch them, unnerved me. I wanted to access their insides on the most primitive level, to understand them and make myself indelible in their perception of their bodies. I wanted, too, to watch the instability of my presence in their lives unravel them.

I told them yes and added I came because I wanted to make sure they really lived there. They laughed. I told them, too, that their messages helped me feel safe, that I understood what they were putting out in the universe and wanted to match the peculiar intensity. Catherine already had sleep in her voice when she told me that was very nice, but she would appreciate it if I held off on the philosophical chatter until the morning. Katrina whispered that Catherine needed to sleep soon after orgasm or she became a bit of a bitch. I slept with the heart of a watchful rabbit.

14

WE THREE ATE PASTA IN THE MORNING. I read my emails on my phone, including one from my father's attorney. I confirmed I could meet him Saturday at noon to review and submit my statement. I opened my app and noticed messages one or both of the wives must have sent during the night, emojis of kisses and tongues and lips. I tried to remember which one had crept out of bed for the bathroom. The night was too blurred. When the wives kissed, I watched and chewed.

I told Katrina I wished she did not have to go into work. She asked us if she should call out sick; with the snow, not a lot of people would come to the store. Then again, she continued, not waiting for us to argue, so close to the holiday, people turned desperate, trying to remember if their spouses wore half sizes or fulls. We nodded.

Don't let me keep you, I said. Is the shift long?

Eight hours, she said and pouted.

I said, You should go, but we'll miss you. They looked at each other and I felt I may have overstepped my use of *we*. I said, What? I was more confident then, and felt free to call them on their stares, the looks they clearly wanted me to notice.

Catherine said, Well.

I said, Well?

Catherine said, Katrina does need to go in today, unfortunately. It's an automatic write-up if you call out without a doctor's note.

I said, Do they even pay for your health insurance?

She said no, she was on Catherine's, so it was all right, but wasn't that unfair to everyone else? Especially because the company forced so many people to be part-time, without benefits.

I said, Jesus.

Anyway, Catherine continued, nodding, Katrina is off this weekend, and I know you weren't wild about the idea the other day, but we thought, Hell, maybe we'll go up to Maine.

I said, Oh! Maine. I felt enormously alone then, reminded that my parents would never be people who invited me for a visit unless it benefited them in some concrete way. I wondered how I would distract myself until the weekend.

Come, Catherine said. Please?

I said, With both of you? I thought of the commitment I had literally just made to my father. His attorney—or an assistant, an Emma, someone who lacked enough dignity to reply within minutes—had already emailed me the details of his office, the witnesses and mediator arranged for Saturday morning. I wanted an excuse not to go, to hurt him, to blow him off entirely, and yet I knew that doing so would not happen without retribution. I thought of how badly Katrina missed her mother, their mutual loneliness. I envied her, and tried to convince myself my father wanted to get out so he could spend time with me.

Catherine said, Well. Yes. She looked at Katrina, whose eyes were bowls of hope.

Instead of mentioning my father, I said, Your mother won't be terribly confused? A lonely woman, I knew, was not necessarily a nice one.

We'll tell her you're a friend, Katrina said. They gave each other that look again. She won't be suspicious.

Catherine said they were going, with or without me, which made me feel queasy despite its reasonableness. She said to take my time to consider it. Though not too much time, she continued. We leave in two days.

Overwhelmed, I gave a mighty cough. I looked to Katrina, who already had her coat on for work. I blurted out that I appreciated her messages, hoping to see her eyes widen, but she only laughed with her mouth, not her belly nor her eyes, the way mothers do. Catherine had pulled a robe over her blouse and I envied its closeness to her body. They were so nonplussed that it seemed likely they really were sending them together. I coughed again, louder, and pretended to be embarrassed. Katrina asked if I'd seen a doctor and I told her no, I didn't trust them much, and she asked Catherine if they should be concerned about getting sick. I don't get paid sick days, Katrina added. Working the floor is miserable with a head cold, much less something like pneumonia.

Catherine told me to open my mouth and I did, happily. I wanted her to tell me I looked perfectly fine, no redness at all, no swelling, no pus. I wanted her to tell me I was a little liar, a little drama queen, a little headache. When she told me she could tell there was something wrong with me, I said, What?

She told me to go upstairs and wait for her in the bathroom connected to their bedroom. I hesitated in the hallway, confused, wondering if I was supposed to kiss Katrina goodbye or not, and she told me she wanted to say goodbye to her wife and didn't know why I was hovering. I cherished being told what to do, the visibility that comes with being embarrassed, though I could not have put my strange happiness into words then.

Once in their bathroom, I masturbated a bit and wondered what I was to do with my underwear once I made the cotton slick with vaginal fluid. After a few minutes, I received a message of several kissing mouths on the app. I returned them, feeling reassured. Oh, I thought. It's her kiss goodbye. I returned to masturbating, my underwear solidly wet, and I told myself to ask Catherine to borrow a pair of hers for my eventual walk home. When she told me from the door to stop that, I did, surprised at her crisp tone, though she had to tell me a second time, louder, for me to actually remove my hand and put it on my lap. I said, I might be feeling better. I realized we had never been alone and wondered what might happen if I pushed past her and dropped myself down the stairs. She would call an ambulance eventually, but how long would she let the two of us be happy and in pain, mine physical and hers emotional? I could not be sure.

Catherine told me I was not feeling better. She kneeled in front of the tub and turned on the water, both faucets, hot and cold. As the tub filled, Catherine asked if I had allergies to anything (no), if I hated any scents (no), and asked me not to do anything outrageous like hold my breath under the water and choke (I agreed that was a reasonable request). With both hands in the water, monitoring, I guess, its heat, she told me to undress myself quickly and leave my clothes in their laundry hamper in the bathroom closet. While in the narrow space I searched for weapons, bloodied rags, hemp or synthetic ropes, dental dams—the usual points of interest.

From her place beside the tub, Catherine told me to hurry the hell up and I ushered myself into the water without making eye contact. The burn went deep. I covered my breasts with my palms and Catherine tugged my hands to my sides. She asked if it was normal for me to bruise so deeply in such a short time and I told her when the bites were all teeth, no lip, it was pretty standard. She said, Ah, and I sensed her lost interest and regretted my honesty. I imagined telling her no, it was unusual, her teeth were special, my breasts were usually heartier but she'd made them malleable, but when she lifted a wet cloth to my face without wringing it, I felt euphoria. I was about to experience a thing, I knew, a new status between just the two of us, though punishment or care I was not then sure.

This will help clear out your lungs, Catherine said. I tried to say, Really? but the water from the cloth shot up my nose, making me cough. Catherine pulled the washcloth back an inch, let me hack myself up, then returned it and kept her hand against my face. With only a little more pressure, she might be able to suffocate me. I leaned forward, let her hand stiffen and cradle my skull, her fingers tight to the edges of my face, and felt in me enormous relief.

The longer Catherine kept me there with her hand and the cloth and its wetness, the smell of soap, no fruit or sugar, just clean, just order, just efficiency, I felt less and less surprised by the wives. I thought, Of course this would happen. I thought, Of course this is precisely what she would do to me and for me. With every surprise made reasonable I felt I understood them more and more.

I missed Katrina, and wondered if she might turn around, might watch the train open its doors and decide no, not today, and walk back home to check on me. Would she be jealous, I wondered, finding her wife keeping me still in quite this way. Would she hit her or me or the both of us. I imagined her nudging Catherine into the tub beside me, still in her robe, and me, naked and bruised, and Katrina's skinny fingers pressing down on our eyelids, keeping us shut. I began to tell Catherine about this fantasy, the awful happiness of it, as loudly and as confidently as I could with a wet cloth on my face, and she let me say it, all of it, even as she drained the tub and I sat there shivering. When we were done, she did not kiss me but she did tell me she would have a surprise for me in Maine.

15

AFTERWARD, STILL DAMP AND COOL BEneath my sweater and coat, I headed to the office still aroused from my bath. I wanted to text the wives and see if I could meet them somewhere this afternoon—a dressing room at the Macy's downtown, so close to where Katrina worked, maybe—but felt too self-conscious, so I resolved instead to procure a present to please them.

Lucky for me, the firm kept gifted bottles of alcohol in a series of low-level cabinets in the kitchen, just below the coffee makers. I knew nothing about hard liquor, as I avoided it under the recommendation of the physician who prescribed me antidepressants. Really, Helen, she told me during a video call when she renewed my prescription for the next three months, don't mess with it. I told her, Sure. I reminded myself of this conversation whenever I opted for cough medicine instead of something stronger than a beer or two or three. I felt abiding by these limitations showed some maturity, some desire to survive in a pleasant way, not bottom-of-the-barrel living but existence with decency and a bit of grace, and I was in the midst of congratulating myself for being responsible when I felt someone approach from behind. I slammed my head on the open cabinet door and cursed.

Before I turned, I heard Emma say, Helen? She stated the obvious: I had been down there awhile and she wasn't sure if my back was acting up. She said, Do you need help?

I dragged myself out of the cabinet and rolled from my knees to my bottom, holding two shapely bottles of what I assumed was expensive scotch. I told Emma I was fine, just tired, and without hesitation, she asked if I'd had a long night, and I heard in her tone she was accusing me of drinking, being generally irresponsible, and I told her yes, but not unhappily, as I'd had a date. She seemed intrigued and surprised me in naming my childhood neighbor and sort-of ex, Amy. No, I said, we haven't spoken in years. I told her I couldn't believe she remembered whatever bit of history I'd dropped however long ago. Emma took some paper towels from beside the sink, balled them up, and told me to cushion the scotch in my purse.

You look sad, I said. With such little encouragement, Emma squatted down beside me and whispered she'd been having a hard time and was, worst of all, bored. As she spoke, I wondered if my boss would wander out and mention how rarely I was in the office, and ran through explanations I could give for taking extreme advantage of our flexible remote work policy. I would mention visiting elderly relatives, caretaking, suggesting, just a little, that I shared in the burden of most women I worked with, who cared for entire families. Emma brought me back when she told me I shouldn't be so wonderful to women if I was going to keep being a player.

I said, Player? I considered telling Emma such casual

rapport was inappropriate but I did not actually care and, in fact, was amused by it. I tried to remember what I had told Emma about myself and came up with little. The most memorable part of our interactions was her curious intensity, though at the time I believed that was a byproduct of her being younger than me, and smarter, and altogether more eager to prove herself as a solitary force. I, of course, recognized in her the desire for the impossible: to be both known and loved.

Emma named a few women I'd mentioned to her. The campaign staffers, the surgeon, the librarian. Her queer attentiveness flattered me; I found myself impressed at her memory and wondered how far back it went. That she might remember too much—all of those trips to the bathrooms and closets— concerned me only briefly. I understood her conscientiousness as desire and wanted her to show me more. I told Emma she must be a good partner, being so attentive, and she looked satiated. She asked if I was bringing the scotches to whomever I spent my date with and I told her I was. Then, feeling I owed her a little honesty, perhaps because I pitied her, and perhaps because I still wanted to intrigue her, to impress her, to make myself feel desirable, I told her there was a special woman who would get it first, even if only a sip, even if only with a splash of tap water. Emma was quiet for a bit, a moment, more or less, and then she told me she was grateful for me.

I said, Grateful? She told me it meant a lot to her to be listened to. She appreciated that I didn't interrupt her during meetings, not even the virtual ones, when she didn't always know when to stop talking. I can chat forever, she said, and I just want someone to tell me they agree, they understand me.

I did understand Emma, though, in truth, I didn't interrupt her or anyone during meetings because I hardly listened.

She told me she felt she could tell me anything and I would understand. I told her that might be true. If I didn't care about losing my income, I would have kissed her then, or put my hand on one of her breasts, or asked her to open her legs, but I really wanted to keep my bank account where it was at, so I told her I had to get moving on the scotch before my lady in waiting lost her patience.

A few minutes later, by the office door, Emma asked me to tell her about the lady. Just one thing, she said, and because I understood the desire to have a secret, to know a little more, to feel smarter, to be chosen, I told her the woman was older, much older, but hadn't lost her love for drinking. Emma repeated *older* and gave me a look like she understood what I was getting at and I was distracted enough to believe I'd done a good thing, that I'd gone and settled what was in the air.

16

AT THE NURSING HOME, I HEATED UP several cups of macaroni and cheese in the staff's microwave. When it dinged, I stirred in the packets of cheddar. I asked my grandmother if she liked the colors. Look at the noodles, I said. So bright. She giggled, happy with the knuckle of scotch and water I had slipped into a paper cup.

My grandmother was my favorite drinker and I grew up recycling her cans of light beer for nickels (with some anxiety, aware that ten-year-olds should not do such things) and enjoyed sneaking her bits of fancy liquor when I had the chance. Only a little at a time, because of her medications. I'd remembered two empty bottles of a similarly expensive-looking scotch by the wives' recycling, and I thought they might appreciate knowing I had spent this time with my grandmother. When I was done arranging her lunch tray, my grandmother shook her cup; I topped her off and she gave me a wink, like I was a little girl and easy to love again.

If my grandmother recognized the macaroni was artificial and heated by a machine, she did not seem bothered by it.

Between sips, she looked at the bowl with a wonder that humiliated me. The gratitude in her eyes reminded me I was a fraud, an imposter. Eat with me, she said.

I ate earlier, I said, my stomach filled with cough syrup. I squatted beside her, as I did whenever she ate. I asked how her hands were feeling. Do you need help today?

I might need a little help, she said, shy. This afternoon she was in a yes mood. If I asked, Do you want to watch TV? she'd say, Of course! If I said, Do you want me to help you into your wheelchair so we can sit in the fresh air? she'd say, Certainly! If I said, Should I break you out of this place? she'd say, Always! If I said, Do you love me? she'd say, Yes, yes, yes. I never asked her the impossible: Do you think my parents should rot in jail for what they did to you.

Feeding an adult is not difficult. The first times my grandmother and I did this, I trembled. I did not watch her chew or swallow. I thought, This is not the way old age should be. I thought, What about dignity? Lack of autonomy is not good or fair. Dependence generates fear. Help, too, breeds happiness. How lovely to say you would like a little help and to receive precisely that.

Most of her teeth were missing. That had been true since I was a teenager, when she had several pulled at the dentist. With better insurance, she might have saved more of her natural teeth, but that was no longer an option. Before my parents had access to her bank accounts, she had spent the bulk of her savings on dentures. Never had I seen her smile so widely. In the nursing home, the dentures spent some days in a case on her bedside table. Others, the dentures greeted me from her mouth. No schedule except, I imagined, the patience of an aide. The missing teeth made finding the right angle for the spoon easier, but I stayed gentle. I did not want to harm.

When she was done eating, she told me I was a very good girl and she loved me. Such a joy, she said. We held hands over the table. She started to cry. Like her dentures, her crying followed no pattern I could decipher. Maybe dementia made emotions come easier, looser, with less consideration. If I grew that old, I imagine I would not cry, but yell myself hoarse. I would be banned from such a place. No one would mind my gums when they spooned me macaroni.

The first few months of our visits, I became red and panicked when she cried, wiping her tears with tissues she kept on her bureau. That afternoon, I let the tears stay. I let her be. She kept telling me I was good, so good, and finally, I told her I was not. I'm sorry, I said. But I am not good.

You are, she said. You are my favorite.

I said, You are my favorite too. But I'm not good. I thought of Emma and her praise earlier that day: what a good listener I was, how patient, how attentive. I felt I deserved none of those compliments.

My grandmother said, Tell me why you're a bad girl. She is in a yes mood, I reminded myself. She will accept everything I say.

I said I could not begin. She looked very serious then and I said, If I started telling you all the bad things about myself, you would never hear the end of it. I pulled a smile and thought she might laugh but she did not. She told me to tell her why I was talking like that.

Right now, she said. Tell me.

I pressed my forehead to our hands. Her skin smelled of lavender. I kissed her knuckles. Beneath the skin, her joints sat like knots. When she was raising my father, she worked part-time as a telephone switchboard operator. How fast her hands must have moved, how nimble. You connected a lot of people, I said. When you worked the phone lines. Do you remember that? You probably connected families and couples and people falling in love.

Yes, she said, I did good things. She bent forward to put her head on mine. Her spine was bad and the lean was tough on her. I scooted forward to help. She said, See? You are good.

I said, Grandma. Do you remember when Ryan and I were kids?

She said, Oh. I miss that Ryan. And you!

I said I missed him too. My words came small, and if she understood me, it must have been by predicting what I would say, not from hearing any intelligible sound. I said, Do you remember when he got sick? When we were kids?

She said she didn't remember him being ill. I repeated my questions and she said, Helen, honey, I don't remember it. She gave me a moment of quiet, then added, Do you? And I realized I wasn't the only person in my family looking for facts amid stories.

I said, You remember my name? I raised my head and she raised hers, the connection rumpled. I said, You always call me by a different name. I did not want to say my mother's name and risk upsetting her.

She repeated my name three or four or five times. I get

confused, she said. Because your mother is the only visitor I had for a while.

I said, You remember my mom coming by your house.

She said, Oh, yeah. She came by a lot, when you were at school and your daddy was working. He was doing the lobster boats then, you remember? A hard worker, my boy.

I said, Yes. I did not know when my father had been let go; he was ill and inconsistent, and they had few qualms firing seamen with his struggle. I did not want to upset her memory of him, and so I said, Mom came by to take care of you, yeah?

She said, Can you kiss my baby doll?

I kissed the doll. I said, Gram.

She said, Mmm?

I said, Do you remember when I said I wouldn't call anymore? You know, because of my parents. I was trying to teach them a lesson, or whatever. Set boundaries around money.

She said, Yes! Cheerful and afraid.

I said, You do remember?

She asked me to kiss the doll and I did. She said, You work in an office now, my big shot.

I tried to forget the marginal contributions I brought to my job. I said, Grams, I thought other people would step in. Anyone.

She said, Do you need an adult to step in?

I told her I was fine, I wasn't the one who needed help. Gram, I said. You needed a lot of help before, and no one was really giving it to you. My mom and dad weren't really taking care of you, and I was cut off from everybody, to prove my point. That's why you're here. You know that, don't you?

Helen, she said, you really need a lot of help. I wondered if my face had begun to bleed. My nose hanging from my nasal cavity. Eyes out my sockets. Molding undone to reveal a rumpled foundation.

I said I didn't need help. I said, Did Ryan need help? My grandmother sat before me in a bed with white sheets and a pink throw blanket. Beyond her, dead Ryan sat with snot dried on his upper lip. I did not wipe his nose, as I did not know how to love him in that way again, but I told him to, and using my sleeve, he did. I wondered where our childhood clothes were, if my parents kept anything after his death. Ryan wore a lot of my shit, hand-me-downs. I wondered, for the first time, if my parents had qualms about this gender swap. My purple crewnecks. My denim overalls. Around the house, we wore the same socks, dingy, with lace around the ankles. I wondered if my parents thought of us at all.

I barely saw you kids when you were young, she said. Your dad wanted you all to live with me, and I was afraid. Isn't that terrible? she said. I was afraid of my son living back home.

I said, What do you mean, afraid? I wondered if she was a little drunk.

I don't want to upset you, she said. But your daddy made some mistakes. He had bad friends, and they ran around, you know what I mean? You don't remember. I did not tell her that I certainly did. She said, And so I didn't want you all to move in, because I thought he wouldn't stop, and then we'd all be stuck.

I asked who watched me and Ryan that winter. Her face was still happy, easy. Our conversations had not been so coherent in years. I did not understand.

No one watched you, honey, she said. You two were good at home.

I said, We were little, Grandma. We weren't home all alone. Right?

You had each other, she said. And I was thinking of you. And your parents were loving on you, from whatever they were up to.

Running around town, I said, while we were home alone. I thought of my father overwhelmed, afraid of the responsibilities he did not know how to handle. I imagined him sitting in the waiting room of the local clinic, holding a thin tissue to my brother's mouth as he hacked himself up. I imagined him at the bar, running a tab, and running out when the registers were closing for the night. I imagined him getting yelled at by the cops because he fell asleep in an alley with his dick out again, piss deep in his jeans. I imagined my father calling my mother, then me, then even sick Ryan, stupid, annoying, ridiculous, unreasonable, cunts. Sitting beside my grandmother, I realized I was not imagining so much as I was remembering, that I was finding some of what I was always looking for— answers, memories, realities I'd outgrown. I felt closer to my decision—would I, wouldn't I—and still uncertain. Guilt has tremendous sway.

Small things happen, she said. You can tell them goodbye.

These are not small things, I said. Gram, you remember what I'm talking about? Ryan was so sick, he didn't get better.

And you. She held my eyes. You're here, I said. You know what I'm saying, don't you?

She said, Helen, you need a lot of help.

I said I didn't. I imagined slamming my mouth against the arm of her bed. My lips would rupture and, depending on the angle, my front teeth. I wondered if teeth could shoot up and reach my eyes from below. No, not everything in the body is sharp.

Small things, she said. Small.

I asked what could be bigger than this. If these things are small, I said. I don't understand what is big.

All the small things make a big thing, she said. You can thank them and then you put them to sleep.

I wanted to scream. I said, I find that very hard, Grandma. How do you make it easy?

She said, I don't make it easy. She said, I have a lot of time to think.

In here?

Alone, she said. She asked me to change the doll and I said, Of course. I stood up and went to the bureau. As expected, her dresses waited in the piles I had left them in. Comfort in routine is rarely overrated. That day, I chose a maroon dress with a white collar. Dignified and studious. I felt the front of my skull separating from my head. I thought, I might die in here.

I asked her what she would do if my father asked her to speak about him. To my grandmother, in her little bed, I said, What would you say? Sway me, I thought. Remove the choice. I wanted to give my brain a rest while my body acted.

She told me she loved me and her doll. I repeated my question and she stayed sniffing the doll's head. I said, Gram, do you think my father is a good man or a bad man? I was worried she might cry or throw her doll at me or knock her tray to the ground. I imagined her spitting in my eyes and decided I would keep them open. I had only a day to decide between my father and the wives. Understand I wanted all or nothing: no rescheduling, no actions with maturity attached.

My grandmother said, He's just like you. I told her no, that wasn't right. Unable to admit the truth, I told her she meant we looked alike; I was all him, none of my mother, in the face. But she told me no, she knew what she meant, and to be a good girl and listen. She put her hand to her chest and said, In here, girl. Identical. You, me, and him. Then she told me to go into her bedside table and grab some cough drops for the road. I shoved four into my mouth and smiled, the purple drops appearing, and my grandmother told me I looked like I did as a little girl: powerful, with a secret.

Hours later, alone on my kitchen floor, I fantasized about my grandmother greeting her son, and me, and herself: big smiles shut eyes wide hugs with hunched shoulders. My apartment was cold enough for the floor to hurt my feet but I told myself I could not get up until I was good. I typed a nice letter, describing my father's extra shifts serving meals in the cafeteria, his regular calls, and his growth. He now asked how I was doing, something he hadn't done before this round of incarceration. He listened, or pretended to, when I shared about my life. He hadn't called me a dyke or a carpet muncher or asked if any of the neighbors, male or female, had shoved their hands down the front of my underwear when I was a kid. No, while my father was serving his sentence, he was the best man he'd been in my life. I sent it to my at-home printer (a perk of remote work) and even found a little envelope, though I planned to deliver it in person. I stood by my kitchen window, let night air roll in a couple of inches, and rubbed my nipples through my shirt. I thought of Catherine, and of Katrina, and of Amy and her girlfriend, and the librarian and her wife, and even, surprising myself, of Emma. I could not have felt I was a better person.

17

SNOW HUNG HEAVY UNTIL WE CROSSED out of Massachusetts, the envelope folded three times to fit in my good pocket on the coat. In New Hampshire, about thirty minutes before I was scheduled to meet with my father's attorney, I lied and told Catherine I was fine with flakes on the windshield and the street. In fact, I preferred it. That January, the trees were bare except for snow and birds. I drove with my hands and shoulders tight, my elbows pinned to my torso. Katrina manned the radio and insisted on local stations instead of a playlist. Seasonal joy to help our seasonal depression, she said. I wondered how much sadness the wives really had in them and how much darkness they would let me witness.

I think I can make it the whole way, I said. Catherine was not shy about questions, nor was Katrina subtle with her side glances, all eyebrows and tunneled lips, but I knew they did not want to rush my explanation of why I interrupted their recent dinner. Like a house cat turned feral, I was greeted with warmth and comforted by the open door and its promise of departure. In the rearview mirror, I saw

Catherine nod and take a sandwich folded in paper out of the cooler.

As I drove, I listened to the shuffling of napkins. Katrina twisted herself backward to face Catherine; I did not trust myself to turn and see that lovely stretch of her neck, as at that point, I did not want to kill us. When she settled back into her seat, she showed me a plate with two sandwich halves. This is hummus and some cucumbers, she said, pointing to a stuffed piece of pita bread. And this, she continued, is a peanut butter and jelly we put on the panini press this morning.

Peanut brittle, Catherine corrected from the back. We have a third sandwich too, a grilled cheese with brie and pears.

For me, I said, wondering if the last woman they dated, the scotch drinker, was sometimes vegan as well. When I passed them the unopened bottle and explained why I chose it, they looked at each other, quiet, until Katrina confessed the bottle was actually from the woman they'd been seeing before me. At seeing my face fall, Catherine told me the experience was a good one, as it helped them decide they did not want to deal with women who drank. They agreed they hated cleaning up vomit, and did not want a partner who was that kind of a mess. The one in the photo, I said. Yes, they said.

Well, Catherine said, whatever you want is yours.

I said, Whatever I want? I wanted whatever distraction the wives could bring. I wondered if they'd packed any rope and if the ceiling beams of Katrina's childhood home were sturdy enough to lift two of us at a time. I wondered if there was a working fireplace, if I could convince Catherine to hang me up and start a flame, nurse it, then yell about smoke and usher Katrina outside in only her underwear. The comfort I imagined at them coming back inside, the house being fine and me having been stuck inside all along, was the bliss I never experienced in my lived life but welcomed all the same.

I watched Catherine roll her eyes. She thought this banter was all in her hands. She said, Try us, before unwrapping the grilled cheese and biting into it. I glanced at the car clock; it was barely noon. I nestled deeper into the driver's seat, momentarily satisfied, until I imagined my father waiting.

I wondered if he had eaten lunch yet, if he'd been served corn from a can or vegetables thawed into edible. I wondered if his proximity to release made the food taste better. His attorney had not yet called him with the news, I figured, and I wondered how long it would take them to decide I was just a shit person, a disappointment, an apple at the base of a tree. I fantasized lightly about hearing my name on the radio, that a report had been issued for a missing woman.

Wanting to feel loved, and to test the wives, I said, Feed me? I'd taken a handful of decongestants before the drive and felt ready to kick out the windshield. Food, I thought, might distract me.

Catherine bent her wrist around my neck and pressed food to my mouth. I opened and let my tongue drop to make room. The bread was coated with a jam or a jelly, something sweet and spicy, and when I chewed, cheese stretched across my mouth. I said, Holy shit. The jam was more tart than sweet, a mix of berries I could not identify. I could separate nothing into its original state: What did a blueberry taste like, a raspberry, a plum? If there were moments I had sat and contemplated the sweet juice of a solitary berry, my mind already replaced them with the haunt of a medley's pleasure. I opened my mouth and said, More, please.

The jam really adds something, Catherine said, confirming my assumption that they knew my thoughts in advance. More bread, more cheese, more jam. I wondered how many sandwiches she'd made, if perhaps she fit a dozen folded into pockets inside her cooler. I hadn't checked the trunk; maybe Catherine had filled it with ice. Maybe we would drive and be fed and not stop until I fell asleep at the wheel and killed us. If I survived, I thought, I might end up in the same facility as my mother. I widened my eyes. Catherine said, Brace yourself, and I did.

In the rearview mirror, I saw her seatbelt was strained. If I stomped the brakes, the jolt would not kill her but it would hurt her. If a moose sauntered into the road, Katrina and I would be injured, and Catherine would likely die. I suckled her fingers, kept her where she was. Her wrist pressed my nostrils closed. Cheerful, I realized we were playing a game. She took her hand away and scratched Katrina's scalp. I said, Now that's all I'll ever want.

Some elderberry should top you off, Katrina said, and I was surprised at her smooth redirection. Their attention thrilled me all the more in that they still saw me as sick, feeble, needy. As Katrina spoke she did not look at me but ahead, taking in snow and shivering trees and gray gray gray from sky to concrete. I wondered if she saw the world as it was or as it appeared to me: dead dead dead. I wondered if my father's attorney had called him yet, had used polite legalese until my father got confused, irritated, and the lawyer finally told him I'd blown the appointment off. To test them, I promised the wives I was better.

No, Catherine said. You're not. I told them I'd hardly coughed the whole drive, delighted and energized at their attention. Catherine told me I'd said the syrup helped last time, and though I knew I had said no such thing, I told her she was right.

Katrina unscrewed the bottle and poured the syrup into the small white cap. She held it out in front of my face and smiled at me like somebody's mother.

That's not funny, I said. It could spill. Catherine asked why I didn't want it, what with my cough and the frigid temperatures, and I told her I did not want to waste their good. You'll get frustrated with me, I said, for once being entirely honest and transparent. Even in my sense of invincibility, the vulnerability made me feel nauseous. I let myself believe fluid and pus really had taken root in my lungs. I imagined the wives ordering me to pull onto the side of the road, removing their underwear, and taking turns pouring syrup into each other's vaginal canals, letting me lap up the drippings. What is a symptom if not a compulsion the mind cannot resist. In real life, I said I didn't want to make a mess in their car.

The wives shared a look I could not entirely see, what with my eyes on the road in front of us, and Katrina lowered her window and dumped the dark liquid into the air. I said, What the hell?

Catherine opened her door. I repeated myself, pitched, and she told me if I wasn't going to accept good things, they would disappear. I said, Close the damn door. I said, Holy fuck. The wind entered the car and curled up inside of my stomach. There were few cars on the highway at that hour, as most people drove on Friday evenings to have a full day of skiing. Catherine asked if I was going to be good or not and I said, Holy shit, yes. She closed the door and when Katrina's hand returned to my face, I opened my mouth and drank the syrup. I even gave a smile. Then Catherine told me to remove my boots.

I said, What? I would have done many things to keep them from leaping from their own car but I did not believe, not entirely anyway, that they would do so. I loved their tests, the thrill. I thought, What is love if not these dips into someone else's nightmare.

She said, You heard me. From beside me, Katrina offered to help.

I'll hold the wheel while you take your shoes off, she said with a hand in front of her mouth. Without waiting for a reply, she leaned over, hands still wearing jams and crumbs, and commandeered the wheel. She nodded at me as though I were a nervous child, and I laughed loudly, too loudly, and felt I was eleven or twelve again, teased, the girl with the dead brother and brain-dead parents, always a step behind on the joke. The wives did not laugh with me.

You're wasting so much time, Catherine said with a wink toward her wife in the rearview mirror. In the car's quiet, I heard her chew and felt a tang of rejection. Me next, I was thinking. Me next. But when she put her eyes on me, she was back to stone.

I made excuses, as one might imagine: That's too dangerous; it isn't funny. What if a cop races by? Can't we do this when we're inside? What if your hand slips, what if my knees jerk around? We don't want to die, do we? The wives mocked me, repeating my questions back to me in their easy unity, and I realized for the first time they might be as fine with dying as I was. Outside, snow contained itself in the sky and mockingbirds took flight. Knees to my chest, I undid my ugly boots and started to tell them they cost only a few dollars, and as Katrina held the wheel, Catherine put a hand on my mouth. I kissed her skin, so happy and so afraid.

18

KATRINA'S MOTHER WAS NOT AT THE house. I asked if that was strange. I'll admit, I felt nervous then. During the drive, I had asked if they needed to call and update her on our trip, but Katrina shrugged it off. She'll be relieved when she sees our faces, she said. We were only two hours away then, half done with the journey, and I still had not given driving privileges to Catherine. Standing in the front room of an empty house, it occurred to me they may have given me such freedom to suggest a power I did not actually possess.

My phone did not have service in the house and I felt relief that I would not hear from my father for some time. The foyer was wide and open, leading straight into a sparse living room. A large and thick-screened TV took up most of the far wall. Beneath it, a handful of hardcover books, framed photos, and Red Sox memorabilia. I realized Katrina, in spite of now selling shoes, had grown up in a home with extra bedrooms. When we removed our boots, we arranged them on a rack to dry. The shoes stacked there already were all sizes.

In a loud whisper, I said, Do you think she's asleep? All around us, quiet.

I'm not sure, Katrina said, her face hidden from me as she undid the loops of her wool scarf. Let me go look around.

Catherine told me to give her my snow-wet coat and I did.

I asked, Are you close with your mother-in-law? Catherine ignored my question, as I expected she might, and stepped forward. She kissed my hairline. In their doorway, I wanted them on either side of me, patting my wet hair, which, after my morning shower, had frozen and then melted on our journey. I wanted to hear, Darling, you've done a good thing but the wrong way. All it took for me to betray my father was a couple of near-strangers fretting over my risk of running a fever; I did not stop to even put the letter in the mail. But that wasn't really it. Even if the wives had turned me away, changed their minds, canceled the trip, or at least my place in it, I would have gone home and eaten crackers and drank syrup and rubbed myself to sleep, letter still in my pocket. Traveling with the wives only fed my hope that I could be a bad person and experience good things.

Catherine removed her mouth from my head and asked for my gloves. She added that I needed to forgive her if her wife was a little much; she described Katrina as obsessive. I hope it's not cloying, she said.

I thought this was Catherine's way of addressing the messages and told her I enjoyed every opportunity to be seen. I hoped for a kiss, or at least a smile, but Catherine only snapped her fingers and so I removed my right glove, then my left. These were not sleek driving gloves. These were grim black numbers a little loose at my fingertips. I wanted to stop but watched her begin to rub her nipples through her blouse. I kept going. I removed my sweater from the thrift store, scratchy and warm and lilac, and I tugged down my jeans. I needed to undo the button but not the zipper. Catherine moved both hands inside her shirt. I stepped out of the pants and left them in their pile on the floor for a few moments. From the floor, I sat in my socks and underwear and bra and watched her fold my things.

She said, And the rest?

I shifted to my knees and pulled my underwear to my ankles. The pair I wore that day was black, high cut at the thighs, and rose nearly to my belly button but not quite. For its small windows, that living room got excellent light. I stretched the underwear and noticed the shimmer of a glob of vaginal discharge coating an old stain. Catherine paused her rubbing and I squatted and passed the underwear up to her. She accepted them with her teeth before dropping them down the front of her shirt.

She said, Thank you.

I hesitated when it came to removing my bra, thinking she might come around and unclasp the back for me; I hoped she would use her teeth and chew my vertebrae, but she did not come forward. My nipples were erect, obviously, with the temperature and my arousal. I kept my socks on and said, This floor is so cold, Catherine. She said she understood.

Katrina entered the living room from the kitchen wearing floppy slippers. When she saw me, she squealed. She approached me with her arms stretched out in front of her, hands and fingers steadied, and I turned my chest toward her so she could grab my breasts. As she grasped them, she said, How darling are you!

I said I wasn't sure.

Catherine closed the space and put her arms around Katrina and me. I said, I guess your mother isn't home, and Katrina told me no, it didn't appear to be so. I asked if I should rush getting dressed, then, should she come through the door. Katrina said I could take my time, which frightened me more.

Noises from the street did not permeate the house. Katrina left us embraced for some time before returning from the upstairs with a thick robe, which Catherine then told me to slide my arms into. When Katrina tied the front, I kissed her neck. She said, There! Much warmer. I did not know how to identify the temperature of that day or that period in my life. I thanked them both loudly. I said I felt dizzy and returned to my squat on the floor.

I thought, wouldn't it be funny, the three of us trapped. Wouldn't it serve me right, the evil in me, to bring myself to an isolated area, far from what I understand, to wait out my time in a chilly space. Our trip involved no paper trail, I realized. The car wasn't a rental, so a company would not come looking for it. I wasn't expected back in the office; yes, eventually, my boss would realize I stopped logging in to my work email, that my contracts and reviews were missing. He would grow livid, but would he call the police? That could take a week, I thought. And how would they connect me to the wives? Phone records, eventually. But none of that would be immediate. I felt relieved that I did not have a pet at home waiting for me. My visits to my father and grandmother would be permanently suspended. That is when I revealed myself with my face; I could not see myself—there were no mirrors hung around the living room—but from the look of the wives, I knew they saw and understood my shame.

Catherine said, Helen?

I curled my shoulders into my torso. I felt my ribs in my chest. Catherine took me to one of the couches. My weight dropped in, easy, and I believed I was any of the people who had laid there before: Katrina's mother, or father, if they existed, if they had ever stepped into this house, if Katrina was born from something so ordinary as parents. Catherine dragged my feet and legs up. I did not resist. I thought I saw my mother in the window, her face red from cold, and pushed aside guilt at not inviting her inside: That's what you get, I thought. For what you did. Even half-awake, my anger is that of a child's.

I asked them not to leave me, and they said, Of course not, and then they walked away. When I awoke, I heard voices in the kitchen.

19

FROM THE COUCH, I GRIPPED MYSELF INTO a ball and turned to face the doorway. I felt a girlish relief in hearing them discuss dinner: two types of potatoes, vegan and regular butter, both salted, how could we not want that flavor, health experts be damned, and in the morning, we would make waffles. I wondered if someone would go buy me canned cinnamon rolls if I pleaded. I stretched my legs and felt a pile against my feet. The wives had left me clothes that were not mine—a thick-knit sweater and loose sweatpants. Inside the bottoms, cashmere. Or fleece? I could not tell. The underwear, black lace. I smiled realizing they'd left me no bra.

After I dressed beneath the blanket, I guessed the pants were Catherine's and the sweater Katrina's. The underwear I could not tell. The pair appeared new. No threads tugged out of order. No discoloration in the crotch. I stood in the kitchen only a second or two before I was noticed. Katrina's mother turned to me and said, You must be Helen.

I said, That's what I've been told! A long wood table had been set with four places. Unlike the ones in the wives' kitchen, these plates were enormous and mismatched. Spring pastels in lemon and lime, one dish with black and white checkers, and the last, mine, I recognized intuitively, a purple resembling a bruise. Steak knives and forks sat on paper napkins beside each plate. In the center of the table, two bottles of dark red wine and a pitcher of water. No ice, no leaking. The daisies in the centerpiece looked real but I was certain they were fake. At the table, Catherine sucked a lollipop.

Katrina's mother laughed like I'd been witty. Between her hands, a red dish towel. Her arms were out when she asked me if I wanted a hug. From behind her, Katrina explained I was not touchy-feely. She tugged the hem of her sweater down and out, stretched the modal away from her stomach. Teenagers act like that, I thought. Embarrassed by their parents, and loving them too. And myself, awkward and hovering in the doorway, unsure of where to put my body, how to blend into a safe person's life.

To her mother, I said, Sure. Up close, I realized the dish towel had a poorly embroidered white duck near the hem. Her mother smelled like cigarettes and salt. Like Katrina, her mother was taller than me. I thought, I have devoured your daughter. I thought, I was naked in your living room. I said, Did you make that towel?

She pulled back enough to look at it, still keeping me close, and I wanted to tell her I loved her but resisted. Katrina, you made this one at camp, she said. Didn't you?

Katrina pretended to look at it seriously, then shrugged. Even with her daughter close, Katrina's mother did not let go of me. I wondered if she'd seen me on the couch, covered in the blanket and the robe. Had the wives told her about my crying? Did they sense my fears? Not of their lies, but of my own.

You were very moody those summers, her mother said. I'm pretty positive you brought this home one August.

I thought, You must really love her, to remember that, and when both Katrina and her mother looked surprised, all smiles, the same face, I realized I had spoken out loud.

During our meal, I could not stop thinking about my father. Was he asking his attorney about me? Did his lawyer deliver the bad news or was it an assistant, a paralegal, an administrator who called? I imagined Emma making the call, though of course, she did not. Did someone say I disappeared, I was busy? Did they suggest I called with an excuse, or did they deliver the truth: I hadn't called, emailed, texted, sent a carrier pigeon? I merely left him. I wanted food to distract me, to fill me, and only when I neared sickness did I get my wish.

Katrina's mother called me a good eater. In my anxiety tunnel, I had been swallowing heaping spoonfuls, mostly of buttered potatoes. Katrina kicked her mom under the table. It's a good thing, her mother said. I didn't think she'd clear half the plate. Encouraged, I spooned seconds of the potatoes. Later, I would find a thick red line around my distended gut.

After dessert, we four held our bellies at the bottom of the stairs. Katrina's mother said to me, You really are so darling in my sweater.

I said, Yours?

She said, Yes! The wives nodded.

Katrina said, I thought the bigness would look sweet. With six approving eyes, I felt the heat of acceptance. I wondered if I could stay feeling like a good small girl forever, or at least until morning.

Upstairs, we had a full mattress, narrower than the one Katrina and Catherine had in their home. I stared at an empty bunk bed across the room. The wives kissed my back; the unity was the point.

The wives patted my butt and I turned over. I did not want one or both of them to feel that she had to speak for me to move, and risk Katrina's mother at the door, asking if we needed anything, hot milk or more meatloaf. So I went to my back. My head below the pillows, the wives at my sides. We left the overhead light on, a normal light surrounded by a grand, carved medallion on the ceiling; I thought, Gargoyles. In the dull bright, I felt appropriately hidden.

I put my mouth on Catherine's breasts, one, then the other, while Katrina masturbated. Katrina's knees bent up, my legs flat out. Catherine kissed my forehead until I closed my eyes, and Catherine squatted beside us. After some time, Katrina rearranged herself and started going down on Catherine. Catherine moved the two of them a few times, scooting legs in either direction, and eventually took a pillow out from behind me and placed it beneath her hips. There, she said. Perfect. I kept my mouth on her breast the best I could in all the shuffling.

Catherine directed Katrina to grab a vibrator out of one of their bags. I could not see which one as I did not want to twist my neck and lose my grip on her breast. They went back and forth about which one was charged, and Katrina brought out one she described as the really great tangerine one, as well as the blue one, which they both agreed was a bit much in the suction but I would likely appreciate it. Because of your thick hood, Katrina said to me as she scooted behind me on the bed. I nodded my thanks and Catherine waved me off of her.

From my new position on the floor, I watched Catherine adjust the vibrator against her vulva. She spread her thighs and shifted her hips back and forth against the duvet cover before Katrina passed her a small, square pillow. Katrina massaged Catherine's shoulders while I stared at her hands as they parted her labia and tugged at her clitoral hood. This one has suction, she said. It's like oral, but nicer.

I said, I'm right here! I laughed a little and the wives did too, pitying me. I was thinking of Katrina's mother, of how happy she was to feed me. I wondered if she would kiss my belly, if she'd want to photograph the pink lines left from the borrowed pants. I wanted the wives to shock me out of my thoughts of family, of the guilt I felt circling me, and yet they seemed determined to keep me as an observer. I watched the suction tip glow in the dark as Catherine masturbated. She adjusted the speed of the machine up and down, her thumb easy and forgiving, and when she came to orgasm, I resisted the urge to pull both of them to the floor beside me. Watching happiness has always unsettled me.

When we three were done we lay in bed together. With my face in Catherine's armpit, I said, I have to tell you something.

Catherine peered down at me with one eye concealed by her hand. Katrina said, What? She did not roll from her side to her back or stomach. I expected tension. The room to tilt. Confession always felt to me a pinnacle, a scream. With the wives, it was all very ordinary. Later, I would recognize the unremarkable as a kind of love.

I told them I'd been lying. I insisted my deception was not about them. I've always been like this, I said. Everyone before you has heard it too. I told them I knew this was not a good time, but now. Everything now.

Catherine said, What? She asked if I was actually seeing someone else—Emma, was it?

I told them no. My adrenaline did not generate tears but a desire for movement. I surveyed the room. A tall bookshelf opposite the bed held a handful of old hardcovers with gold lettering on the spines. The shelves displayed more porcelain figures than texts. Their white faces painted in pinks, ceruleans, and seafoams. Yes, I thought. From the top shelf, I could look down and understand. If I tipped, I tipped. Beneath the wives, I did not move.

Catherine said, What? No more alarmed nor angry than before. Her hand left her eye and went to my forehead. I leaned against her palm, pushing, testing, and she pressed back. The pressure helped.

I said, I hurt someone to come here.

Catherine kept rubbing my head. Would it help if we did some guessing?

Could the truth be so easy? I wondered. I said, Yes.

Katrina shifted closer but still did not turn. Catherine

said she would begin. She asked, Is there a body in your apartment? I heard Katrina giggle into her wife's body.

I said, No, it's not like that. I said it wasn't at all like that.

Katrina asked if I had a woman waiting on me. Someone we don't know about, she said. And she's missing you?

I said no. Not that kind of love.

Katrina asked for a hint. I think the hormones scrambled my brain, she said. I can't think.

You remember what you read? I said. About my parents? I didn't wait for a verbal response: of course they remembered; everyone did. But I couldn't get the truth of it out—I started and stopped, My dad, My dad, My dad, until Catherine asked if he had died.

I said no. He wanted my help, I said. And I bailed.

Their faces said they were so sorry, though they, like everyone, had little sense of what in the hell I was trying to express. Familiar and unusual each time.

Can I ask? Catherine said. Is it money or something? Or his lawyer?

No, I said. Not quite. I managed to tell them that my father wanted my help getting parole and they told me it sounded hard, so hard, and I was crying, and they couldn't quite understand me, I was sure of that even then; I was trying to tell them about the letter, how I'd written it and kept it in my pocket, and they were nodding, petting me, and promising me I was still a good girl, their best girl, the very best. Katrina held the sheet out for me and I blew my nose while Catherine held my hair back.

After I quieted, the wives thanked me for telling them. I

said, That isn't enough, that isn't everything. Katrina told me I had a whole life they wanted to hear about, no hurry, plenty of time. I did not expect to wake again during the night, and when I did, I said what I could not take back.

20

WE SLEPT IN A HUDDLE. KATRINA STRETCHED long and could have taken up most of the bed alone. Catherine, as she had our first night together, slept close to the fetal position. Did she curl all the way into herself when comfortable? I hoped so. I stayed on my side but flat. The proximity of their breathing worried me. Would a cough wake them? Pleading? A song? If a spider dropped from the ceiling, would we stay still? A web is a home that thrives for some. I sat up.

Removing myself from the wives was easier than I anticipated. Catherine grumbled but did not wake. Katrina claimed more of the bed in my departure. Abandoning two leaves no one entirely lonely, I told myself.

Beside the bed, I stood and made my confession. I spoke to understand myself, my motivations for wounding my father, for lying to him and to myself. And, as ever, to test the wives. I'm so angry, I said. I have more rage than you could feel. I was not yelling, not raised up in myself, but I was not whispering. These were not mumbles. I said, You need to know this about me. I said, Are you listening?

The wives slept.

I barreled on, transfixed at hearing my weak rationales aloud for the first time. I said, My father sits in a box every day and asks me to do one thing to help him get out. I tell him no, over and over, and he lures me there to talk about my dead brother. Of course, I told them, he doesn't respect my one boundary. He asks me again to pretend he is good and I agree. Mistakes, right. Mistakes. The *s* got lost in my mouth, a childhood tic, the fine humiliation of a lisp.

I continued my stage whisper. I said, My parents are not even bad. They're not even evil. They're not. Neglect isn't even hate, just inaction. And we just let inaction happen. I kept saying, You know, you know, as the wives slept.

I sat on the bottom bunk and continued. I told them I wouldn't help my father because I didn't want to be the only person in our family who hates themselves, that I wanted him to carry some of the shame too. Across the room, one of the wives rustled her feet, then stillness. Confident they were asleep, I told the wives I wanted my parents in jail for as long as they could be held, longer even, because at least they thought of me there. At least I knew they were safe, or close to it, not sleeping outside or in an unlocked car. Not hitting strangers in convenience store aisles. Not snorting in fast food bathrooms. If keeping my parents close meant keeping my parents in a box, I would have pressed my hands on the lid and said goodbye to ever raising my arms.

The bunk beds had white sheets and crocheted throw blankets in colors I could not discern in the dark. On the bottom bunk, my thoughts returned to my mother and father.

What if one fell from the top bunk and split their face. What if one argued for the bottom and a fellow inmate took revenge. I fretted about horrible scenarios born and bred in my imagination: bleach in shampoo, rat poison in scrambled eggs. To make the bad thoughts go away, I rolled onto my stomach and put one hand beneath me. I rubbed myself through my folds, eager for friction. My worries transferred to the blanket: What if vaginal fluid leaked onto this bed? I did not know how the wives planned to wash the bedding. No one had introduced me to the washing machine. Into the pillow, I cried. I told myself to climb the ladder to the top mattress. I wanted to experience all of my parents.

When I woke again, still on the bottom bunk, sun had warmed the room. I checked my phone and noticed I had one bar of service. On the app, a message telling me she wished she could watch my dreams. I thought, My wives are sweet. I wondered which one sent it, or if they had woken in the night to fuck without me, then thought, Hell, leave her a nice note, good enough, why not. The possibility of it being Amy crossed my mind, but I told myself that was the power of thinking backward: my parents, my grandmother, Amy. A circle I wanted to watch spin but did not want to step inside. I was wrong, all wrong, but as I would soon learn, I was close.

Surprise, Catherine said, her face on me from across the room. This room gets excellent light. She added, Funny you haven't coughed since you got here. I gave a cough and I swear I saw her wink. I thought I recognized an unknowing in their faces. I was witnessing, of course, only what I wanted.

21

I IGNORED SEVENTEEN CALLS FROM THE jail before I finally answered back at my apartment. On the drive back to Massachusetts, the wives treated me the same up until the moment they dropped me off; yet I felt a distance start in myself, a walling, a desire to isolate. My confession felt all too vulnerable, too close to a birth for me to know how to maintain eye contact. Even if they hadn't heard it, or pretended not to hear it, I felt raw and bitter, as though they had pulled the truth from me with their teeth. And still I imagined them taking me back whenever I perked up, whenever I felt lonely or drained of happiness. But first, my father.

On the phone, he introduced himself by his first name and I accepted the call, knowing full well what would happen. I said, Hello, and my father said, Helen, what the fuck? You fucking bitch. He said, Why in the fuck would you lead me on? I was counting on you. This whole family was counting on you. Do you have an apology ready or does it need to be smacked out of you?

I said, Dad. I did not tell him I was sorry, though I both was and was not.

My father told me he felt used. He said, Helen. You have always been such a bitch when it comes to anyone but yourself. I'm sitting in here, I'm fucking rotting, you know that? I can't leave, I can't choose my own food. I don't choose when I take a fucking shower. And you let me believe you're actually gonna give two shits about this family and what do you do? You fall off the face of the earth.

I imagined telling my father a number of lies: I'd had an emergency, I'd been in the hospital, I'd been abducted, my rental car had broken down. Instead, I told him I shouldn't have agreed to write the statement, and I was sorry my confusion led to this pain for him. He told me to fuck myself.

Don't fucking come by. Don't ever fucking call me, he said, and I did not point out that I couldn't anyway. He told me he was done with me. His disappointment heightened my survivor's guilt—I wondered, hardly for the first time, why I wasn't the one to get sick and not get better. He told me I was killing him, letting him waste away because I was too busy doing God knows what. You're so selfish, he said, and I heard a man in the background tell someone—my father, I guessed, but I'd never have a way of knowing for certain—to calm the fuck down. You're bad, he told me. You're bad.

I said, Bad what? I asked him to tell me what I was.

You're a shitty fucking daughter, Helen. And granddaughter. You couldn't have fucking come by and helped? His volume reached levels it had not since I was small and lived with both of my parents. You're the worst fucking person I know, he told me.

I said, Same to you. In my body, I made myself as small as I felt—only an odor, only a shaped nostalgia. He told me I should watch my fucking back and I asked him why, a laugh in my throat, finding him ridiculous, until he said my mom was getting out, didn't need shit from me either, and she wouldn't be happy about the drama I'd pulled. He told me she'd be at her sister's place and I recalled it from my teenage years, a tottering colonial in the Boston suburbs. For the first time, I hung up on him, alone and afraid.

Days moved past me and I did not respond to the wives, not even when Catherine or Katrina messaged me over and over on the app in response to my two- and three-second shots of my feet in my dirty kitchen sink. I sensed Katrina was the one sending the messages, and it made me want to punish her even more, for believing that I would give her special treatment over her wife. Hurting others has always been my preferred method of dealing with problems of my own making. In my apartment, I festered. I wore Katrina's mother's clothes over and over. When they were in the washer, I worked. Emma surprised me by emailing a series of links: places we could get catering on the office card, trails we could explore on an hour lunch, videos of kittens grooming dogs. I liked imagining her pasting and erasing, worrying about how I would react to this shift in our communication. I wondered if Emma ever filmed nudes and if I could get her to send me one; I didn't ask, I never did with coworkers, but the wondering gave me back a sense of knowing. This is exactly the sort of person I am, I reasoned. I'm still me.

The anonymous women sent me all kinds of love messages: *baby i missed you babe where did you go angel it's been far too long so glad you're back sweet thing so glad you're okay it's a scary world out there wondered if you'd been arrested ha ha ha imagine that can you imagine darling can you can you imagine.* I reread the messages just in case Catherine sent one in iambic pentameter. (She did not.)

She and her wife did send several ordinary texts, as well as two phone calls I ignored. The wives asked after my sleep, if I was taking good care of myself. They wanted to make sure my cough hadn't turned into a fever: They shouldn't be worried about catching something, should they? They figured I was busy with work and would see me shortly. In a voicemail, Catherine said they wanted me over soon, to talk about happy things as well as hard things. Beside her, Katrina's voice added, That means your family, Helen. I could not explain my self-hatred to the wives, so I ignored them for five days.

22

THE EVENING I PUT MY BREAST IN EMMA'S mouth felt fine, mild, only relatively eventful. The bar had lit its fireplace for the first time since the renovation, and we, like all other patrons who hustled in before six thirty to make happy hour, scooted our round tables close to the flame. Emma insisted on taking the T with me directly from the office, though I advised her to go home and change. I said, Emma, don't you want to be beautiful for me? And she laughed as though I were joking. Too far out of the way, she told me, the first lie. We spent forty minutes on the T, me sitting, her standing in front of me, knees knocking each other's hard spots, and after we exited our station, we steadied each other over black ice until we arrived at the place she tolerated and I loved. When I thanked her for asking me on a date, her mouth fell into a sweet tunnel. She did not close it until I reassured her I was only teasing.

To start, Emma ordered a red cocktail and I drank a light beer quickly. Anything to distract from my guilt of ignoring the wives, anything to distract from the refrain of my father's anger in my head. My mother now seemed ever closer, and I surveyed the bar to make sure she was not at a table or looking in through a window.

The bartender broke the beers' flavor profiles down for me, though I processed only rudimentary sensations: bitter bitter sickly sweet bitter bitter bitter. The bartender's eyes appeared to me as wet wounds and I wondered if she was happy, if she had a place to live on her own or, as I had in my midtwenties, if she lived in a house with five roommates and a mildewed shower curtain. After she asked if I enjoyed the drink for the second time, I reassured her I really appreciated the hint of orange. She gave a friendly grimace and I reminded myself to tip her double.

Does that bother you? Emma said.

I said, What? I passed her my beer. You can try it, I said. I don't care if you're sick.

I'm not sick, she said. I take vitamins. She examined my drink as though checking for backwash or spiders. When she lowered her nose to it, I contemplated placing my palm against her neck and jolting her face into the glass. A mess, sure. A shattering? Unlikely. She added that she drank a berry smoothie every day.

I told her that was nice and asked if she used fresh or frozen fruit. Both, she said. And dried berries. I told her that sounded luxurious, and she told me the bartender was flirting with me. Does it make you feel like meat? she said. It always bothers me, when they do that.

I noticed the bartender hadn't looked at Emma one way or another, but Emma's awareness brightened my mood. I was a full bottle of Dayquil in and afraid of myself. I asked Emma if she was jealous.

Emma said, Jealous? She sipped my beer and scrunched her nose. I took the glass back and drained the liquid close to the bottom. I asked if she wished the bartender had hit on her and she shrugged. When I asked if she missed women, she perked up.

I do, she said. I really do.

I held up a finger to pause our conversation and grabbed a bowl of sweet and spicy peanuts from the empty table beside us. I informed Emma the nuts were free and she nodded forlornly. Go on, I told Emma. Please. Emma described her relationship with her boyfriend, whom she mentioned frequently in the office but whose name I could never remember.

And the bartender, I said. You wish you gave off the vibe too? She said, Vibe?

I said, You know. Gay. Queer or whatever.

Emma appeared to size me up. I straightened my back and checked my fly: zipped. I narrowed my eyes to give off a smolder. I could not remember if I had combed both sides of my hair that morning and gave the length of it a flip over my shoulder. Emma said, You think you give off a real gay vibe, don't you?

I said, Well. I said, Yeah. I'm, you know . . .

Emma said, What?

I said, You know. I looked down at my blouse and noticed sunscreen had stained the collar. I wiggled my shoulders and lowered my chin.

Emma regarded me for what felt like too long of a moment

before she smiled as though I were a small child with a large vocabulary. She said, Oh, you think you're a power lesbian or something?

I said, Well, isn't that why you're always hovering around and following me into the bathroom?

She flipped my phone over to reveal its case. Your phone says *dyke* on it, Emma said. It's probably that with the bartender.

Right, I said, temporarily humbled. I asked, And with you?

With a smile, Emma told me she was obsessed with me. Joking, I assumed. She said we shared an evil and nothing could keep us apart. To test her I said, What about that man of yours? And her sweet face drooped. I did a bad thing then by filling her silence. Don't worry, I told her, I'm only teasing. When I told her I was fine with being a secret she grew old with, I did my little moves: shoulder shimmy, wink in one eye and then the other, in case she missed it the first time. I was laughing and she joined me, ha ha ha ha ha ha ha. I was still laughing when I excused myself to the restroom, two drinks in and processing my anxiety as arousal. A urinal had been repurposed as a planter. Before I pissed, I smelled the orchids: bright, bright.

Sitting on the toilet, I ran through my usual routine: remove my shoes, wiggle my toes to bring life back, and stream my feet while I urinate. The app brought a lot of love that evening, though none from my wives. I wondered if they sensed my proximity to Emma, and I tried to repress my guilt by rubbing two fingers against my clitoris. I wanted to transform my shame into another emotion, to cover up missing the wives by achieving yet another hit of adrenaline. I missed Katrina's wide areolas and the way Catherine turned her head away from me when she groaned. Always giving me another level to ascend to.

Messages relayed what I wanted to hear every nanosecond: *miss you love you perfect beautiful never disappoint good precious valuable unforgettable a gift gift gift*. I couldn't orgasm. With one hand, I wiped and flushed and continued sitting. I was a little drunk and more than a little sad. I worried I'd squandered my opportunity with the wives, though I was not sure, precisely, what that opportunity involved: sex love intimacy trust death an opening. Sex, I figured, my thighs going numb on the porcelain. Likely death.

I refreshed my app and found no new messages. I thought no no no no no no no no. I started filming again, pointing and turning out my feet. I heard the bathroom door open and close and regretted not pushing the trash can in front of it. For a moment, I pointed the camera up to my face, appearing on my stream in dim colors. Up my nose, dark circles gleaming. I'd only been tweezing above my eyebrows for a few months. My face existed in a world outside of my own head. Only a moment.

When I stepped out of the stall to wash my hands I realized Emma was standing beside the sinks with her phone out. She said, Hey. She looked delighted.

I said, Hey. I turned on the sink and asked her to bring some soap over. I wanted to test her, to see if she picked up what I was setting before her. I imagined working my knuckles

into her vaginal canal with her hips demolishing those orchids. People waiting outside, pissing and shitting their pants,
desperate for relief. I let the faucet run very, very hot. I leaned
my forehead against the mirror to steady myself.

Um, Emma said. Sure. She put her phone into her back
pocket and pumped the machine closest to her. We watched
pink liquid drop into her cupped palms. Drip, drip, drop. My
hands felt skinless. When Emma moved beside me and spilled
the soap into my palms, she gasped. Helen, she said. Holy
shit. She turned the faucet off and stayed close.

I rubbed the soap between my fingers. Red red red. I wondered what Emma might look like suckling my bones. I said,
You good?

Emma repeated my name. She turned the water on cold
and told me to hurry getting the soap off. You need to be careful with yourself, she said. You could, like, flay your skin off.

I said, Really?

She said, Obviously, Helen, annoyed, but still close. I considered Emma. Taller than me, and broader in the hips and
shoulders, with features I could never quite recall, her embod-
iment that of a changeling, or rather, a myth. I asked her for a
paper towel and as I dried my hands, I asked her if she would
like a kiss.

Emma reacted to my offer in one of my least favorite ways,
which was to look around as though we were being watched.
I asked if her boyfriend had a habit of lurking in the vents of
bathrooms and she gave me an eye-roll and asked if I wasn't
really missing the woman with the scotch. I asked her what
woman, forgetting myself, always, and she told me the older

woman I'd mentioned that time at work when I stole the bottle. I corrected her: I hadn't stolen it, but taken it, and the woman was my grandmother. She huffed low and deep and I felt a little sorry for confusing her, as I, of course, knew what she was really getting at.

I told Emma to block the door and that no one either of us knew would ever find out. She gave me a hurt look, I think, or perhaps she shared my absolute terror at being seen and understood, and shuffled the recycling and trash cans in front of the door. She hesitated in front of the handle and I wondered if she might actually tip the cans and bolt, but she only turned the lock.

Emma placed her phone against the sink. I have a request, she said.

I said, Sure. I worked my tongue around my teeth, trying to get remnants of peanuts out of my molars. I had heard many requests, especially in my younger years, when I entertained more women with men in their lives. Could we go slow, could she keep her eyes open, could I lead things, could I let her lead, could we choose a safe word, could I say something specific, could she make noise without me getting annoyed, could she stay mum without me stopping and asking what was what, over and over again. Emma surprised me, I'll admit, when she asked if she could film it.

My phone's quality isn't even good, she said. It's just for me. She sounded almost rehearsed but I told myself not to focus on it.

She impressed me with her agency and so I said, Sure. I told her about my live streams, and she didn't hesitate, didn't blink, and I went on and filled in the name of the app and my username too, and she watched me speak, transfixed. She described herself as *familiar* with it, grinning as if she'd won something, but I didn't get it then, not really; I thought I was just being accepted. Only mundane consequences occurred to me: What if the angle was unflattering, what if Emma's files were hacked. What if she began to play the video during a meeting as an accident or a means of lashing out.

Emma squeezed my hips a good bit and I offered to unbutton my blouse. I said, Are you into boobs or not? I learned not to assume with women. She nodded, kissing me again, mouth equally frantic and focused, and told me she could go hairline to toes if that's what I wanted. Despite my camming, I'd only ever let Catherine make me perform in-person. I considered calling Emma's bluff, her too-smooth reaction to my streams, but worried she'd be squeamish about my broken toenails and sweaty arches. Instead, I opened the top three buttons of my shirt. I tugged both of my breasts out of my bra and heard her say, Is it a statement? Like, politically.

I said, What? I looked down too, and squinted. I plucked the nipple hairs of my right breast and not my left. Maybe I had been rushing that morning in the shower, or I lacked an awareness of my body and hadn't retained the mistake at all. I asked if body hair bothered her and she told me no. I told her to relax her face and guided her mouth to my right breast. I felt unmoored from my body, less connected to physical sensation than with the wives, though I told myself to admire the way Emma and I looked in the mirror. I missed Catherine and Katrina and did not quite know where to put those feelings, what to do with myself or the choices I made, and as Emma sucked my breast into her throat, my eyes watered.

I pulled my breast from her mouth and returned both of them to my bra without cleaning off the spit. I told Emma we needed some water and then we could go back to my place. I told her to smell the orchids before we left.

Helen, Emma said. Those are plastic. Then she turned off the video.

23

AT THE NURSING HOME THE NEXT DAY, my grandmother asked me to sleep over. I don't have a bed ready for you, she said, so sad. But you can make one up yourself. Do you remember where the pillows are, in the hall closet? I said, Sure. I did not know if guests were allowed to stay overnight. When I was a kid, my grandmother and I had sleepovers, just after Ryan died. I slept on a cot we dragged into her bedroom, as I could not sleep alone, and my parents locked their door at night. I woke often and put my finger beneath my grandmother's nose to make sure she was alive. My closeness startled her and often caused her to scream. I regretted the panicked turn of her face, still visible in my memory in spite of the dark room, but could not resist my desire to make sure the living lived. Eventually, she let me sleep beside her, even though I was too old for it. I did not think such a circumstance would be possible in the nursing home, but I felt a terrible certainty she would die if I left that night.

The facility did not have cots for guests. We have extra beds, an aide told me. But we can't let you use one. We spoke in the hallway because I did not want to upset my grandmother. When she caught me dragging an armchair from an empty room down the hall to my grandmother's room not twenty minutes later, I expected her to scold me. I wondered if the security officers I'd seen in the lobby were actual police officers. If I disappeared, I wondered, would my grandmother remember who I was and be able to describe me for a missing persons report. Would she repeat my mother's name, over and over, before the staff told her, Sorry, honey, we have no record of her. But the aide only helped me push the chair, unspeaking.

The nurse came in for my grandmother's nightly pain medication, her dinner, her dessert. My grandmother insisted I eat the custard and I did. The yellow was happier than I expected. She ate boiled carrots with her mouth open. I checked my phone and realized I had an email from work; I was to come in for a meeting tomorrow morning, though the reason was not listed. I thought, Shit. I thought, Oh, well.

I checked my phone and saw a number of messages on the app. The texts read as manic, bizarre, sexual, and frightening too—*show show show show show show show*. I was sure they were from Katrina, as Catherine would never be so open in her wanting, so desperate to prod me into her games. The messages made me want the both of them less, though I did not want to admit that even to myself: Who was I without a distraction? Deeper, of course. But who was I without women to make me aspire to be better. I wrote back, *Katrina, are you okay?* I asked her to call me in the morning.

Not long after, I arranged myself between two armchairs, used my coat as a blanket, drank most of a bottle of Nyquil, and slept. Under my coat, I felt very pleased with my foresight. A fashionable coat would not have the fortitude to warm me in a state-sponsored residential home. Not so close to the window, not so close to cold. Just some rest, I told myself, before I do my check. My finger under her nose, a promise, a gift.

24

I CREPT OUT OF MY GRANDMOTHER'S room at close to one in the morning. On my way I checked her tray and side tables in case a distracted aide had left pain medication out in the open. Of course there were only tissue boxes and folded doll clothes. I checked her nose: air in and out. I kissed her forehead. She tasted of skin and soap. I left her a note, thanking her for her hospitality, and sketched several large flowers in blue ink. Her reading ability varied by the day, but I figured the aide would understand. I wondered if my grandmother would miss me in the morning. If she would think it was me who left or my mother. I did not think this was the worst way of leaving someone you loved.

When I saw Katrina in the parking lot, I thought I was finally experiencing a hallucination. I said, Holy shit. I said, Katrina? Catherine and Katrina's car was not so unique to be immediately recognizable, but the lot was nearly empty. Just a handful of cars belonging to staff, plus my rental. Had I not seen her head tilted back behind the wheel, her chin far up in the air, perhaps I would have driven home and been none the wiser. How funny, the way our choices shift our lives.

I knocked on the window and stepped back. From outside, I could not hear Katrina's scream, but I watched her. She lowered the window and said, Helen! I've been waiting for you all night.

I asked her how she found me. She told me she followed me earlier and figured she'd chat with me when I left at the end of visiting hours. I didn't know they let you spend the night, she said. Do you do that a lot?

I told her I had never slept over before. I said, You followed me? She told me it was obviously what I wanted. I gave her a look of disagreement.

I thought you didn't drive, I said. You came here all alone?

I don't, she said. And I did. She said her wife was spending the night in western Massachusetts for a small academic conference. She didn't want to bother with the drive, Katrina said, so she took the commuter rail.

Does she know you're here? I was flattered, and shaken, and I also felt guilty and skittish, wishing they could materialize only as a double.

She doesn't, Katrina admitted. She turned her car on and told me to come around to the passenger seat. I did. I told her I was surprised she was able to sleep. I looked at her hands, worried about frostbite and realized she was wearing Catherine's black gloves. Katrina jolted me back into the big picture and asked me how my grandmother was doing. I told her she was fine, the same, and Katrina asked why I didn't just tell them I was visiting her. Why, she wanted to know, did I insist on dropping off the face of the planet?

I've only known you a few weeks, I said. She gave me a look of knowing, and I admitted I don't want anyone to remember her this way. A delirious old woman who waited for help in her own filth for who knows how long. It's shameful, I said. I'm humiliated.

Katrina offered me the line I had heard again and again: It doesn't make sense, how people could just abandon an old woman. She asked if I talked to my parents since Maine and I admitted I had spoken to my father, that it went poorly, and with my eyes out on the parking lot, as though manifesting my mother from between the lines on the pavement, I confessed that she was out already. Each time I turned a sidewalk corner and did not collide with my mother I felt again abandoned by her; I breathed better too.

What my parents did doesn't make sense, I said. It doesn't make sense my mom got out, and my dad's still in jail, and neither are serving much time. Ryan's name was in my mouth but I didn't say it, as I knew his death did make a kind of sense.

We can hold confusing things together, she said. We're all adults here. To prove her wrong, I told her I wasn't. She ignored me and took a green-and-white box out of the glove compartment. She smacked the pack against the butt of her palm.

I said, You smoke?

She said, Don't tell Catherine. She gave me a wink. I want one pretty bad, she said. But I don't want to stand outside in the cold.

I put my hand on the gearshift. Stay, I thought. Katrina put hers over mine, then moved both to her lap. Beside our hands, her nicotine. My skin warmed between Catherine's gloves, and I wondered if my grandmother sensed my absence, if she'd awaken when I left. If she'd see the armchair, all florals in pastel, and remember my body as a body and not as a dream. I did not know which was less painful—a body or the memory of one. Katrina put her blinker on.

I said, Are we leaving? I looked across the parking lot to my rental. I said, You might as well let me drive, in case we get pulled over. Katrina ignored me and turned the car in a circle so we faced away from the building. Before us, empty lot and shadows I assumed were trees.

You look like you're feeling too much, she said.

I am, I admitted. She told me to tell her what I was imagining—she knew I was leaning into fantasy already, placing myself outside of real life and into my mind—and I said I saw myself split open on the highway, seagulls in from the coast inspecting my insides. She told me I would be easier to handle if I was always so transparent. I agreed, of course, though I did not communicate my assent with words.

Sanitize your hands, she said. There's a bottle in the glove compartment. As I did so, not causing a mess or leaving any evidence of my presence at all, Katrina removed her jacket, unbuttoned her jeans, and waited. We watched my hands flap in the space in front of me to dry the sanitizer faster and she said, Thank you.

Fingering Katrina was not the easiest feat, which was, of course, precisely why she requested it. I leaned over from my seat and used two fingers to massage her mound and vulva before edging across her clitoris. She was not aroused at first and I stilled, asking if she would like anything different or a break. She told me no and to keep going, so I did. I wondered if she, too, was thinking about the three fingernails Catherine left longer for scratches. I didn't dare ask, too afraid of ruining the little moment we had going, and so I worked my wrist harder and dipped my fingertips into her vagina where I was met, finally, with moisture. I thought, Thank Christ. I used my pointer and middle finger to massage her clitoris and the surrounding area until I felt her rock against my palm. I locked my arm then, trying my hardest not to ruin the rhythm. When she orgasmed against my fingers, we did not kiss.

As I cleaned my hand on my jeans, Katrina said, When was the last time you did that? and like a little jerk, I told her I didn't know what she meant, and she said, Sex, and I said, Was that sex? She said, Helen, and I went quiet, guilty, wondering if it would be undignified to talk about the wet mouth on my breast. I was feeling ready to lie up and down to save what I didn't want to lose, and Katrina gave me grace. Though I looked away from her I felt her hope and sadness both, and when she said, Tell me how you feel, I felt such a blessing.

I said, You too. I said, On three.

We counted one, two, three, and in unison said, Empty. I said, I don't know how to respond to your messages. It confuses me because we never talk about them in real life.

She said, What do you mean?

I said, On the app. I don't see them in time to reply and you never mention them when Catherine is with us. I don't even know for sure if you send them together or not.

My use of *with us* felt funny in my mouth, as we were never two but always three. This time in the car felt like an unnatural betrayal. I missed Catherine and her warm cruelty.

Guess it's your secret admirer, Katrina said. I've hardly messaged you on there since we talked on the phone. You were pissed, remember?

I felt sick. I said, You're always teasing. When she looked worried, I sensed she was not joking, and I felt I had been traced, caught, that my footprints were being examined for a race I had not realized I was running. I could not let it go, I said, Catherine mentioned you being obsessive. She wanted to make sure the messages didn't bother me.

Katrina held one pinky in the air. She said, My wife really said that, you're sure? I took her pinky in mine and was surprised by her hand's warmth. I tried to recall what precisely Catherine had said and could only shrug. It's what I understood, I said. She might have been vague about it.

Katrina said, Maybe my wife's playing a little game with you. She laughed and I felt sicker. I asked if she wasn't upset at the thought of Catherine messaging me behind her back and Katrina told me it seemed only one of us had something to worry about.

Later, alone in my living room, I would cram dry crackers into my mouth and see a reply to my last message on the app. The text read, *Katrina, who?* A sad face followed.

25

I'M PUT ON UNOFFICIAL PROBATION AND told if I miss any more work without a doctor's note, I'll be out of the job. No more remote, no more flexibility, no more benefit of the doubt. I questioned the legalities of this but decided I didn't care enough to wonder. After the meeting with human resources, I stomped outside and Emma followed, her curious haunt on me at all times, and she revealed she was worried I had been fired. Fired, I said to her. What made her think that? I was hoping to get a little office gossip, but she said we needed to have a talk and asked if I wanted to get lunch. She put her hand on my forearm before I could say no—this touch felt like our most intimate yet.

The chicken place she led us to was all energy. Inside the restaurant's pink walls, the menu puzzled me in its lack of co-ordination. Ordering a number two, for example, delivered you, as I learned, not two pieces of chicken but three. At the table, I asked Emma, who ordered a number three, if she got four pieces, and she patiently explained she received three. Two thighs and a breast, she said. Because I ordered the num-ber three, she continued, and pointed to the glowing menu as though we had not both stood in front of it and stared, dry mouths open, like two priests about to turn a corner. I nodded and began to spoon mashed potatoes into my mouth. The mushroom gravy burned. Every table for two had a clear vase with a single white flower. Ours looked very alive.

I took the toasted brioche bun off the chicken breast and added my other, impossible, baffling extra piece of chicken onto the first. I shook my head and removed the second. I spooned yellow yellow macaroni and cheese onto the first piece of chicken then returned the second piece on top. I drizzled some red red hot sauce onto the top piece. I drizzled honey onto the bun. I gave Emma a smile she did not quite return. I arranged the bun back on top, used the palms of my hands to press down, and wondered what I was feeling. Exhaustion, I decided. Terror.

Emma rolled her lips into her mouth. She said, Um.

I said, What? In the kitchen, a fire alarm and laughter. I wondered if the employees would let me sit beside the frying machines and funnel good into my skin. What better way to purify one's self than to lodge something solid into one's pores. I fingered my sandwich, considering what I could contain. As Emma explained herself, I bit and chewed and left my body. The burn lived from my teeth down. She asked if anyone in the office had mentioned anything about the internet and I asked what the hell she was talking about.

Well, she said. Please don't be mad. I lied and told her I could never be angry with her. She told me she'd been viewing my streams from her work computer. I said, What. She said it only happened a couple of times—though she managed to save at least one stream with my face and replayed it over and over, she said, because she liked the emotional connection—and she always deleted her history, but she heard from someone in accounting that everything is saved on some master history she can't get to unless someone from IT helps. I thought asking IT might make it worse, she said. You know they're so gossipy.

I said, What?

I'm, like, so sorry, Emma said. I did it when I was a little drunk.

I said, You drink in the office?

Scotch, she said. I stared until she said she was trying to be more adult. I said I could understand that, if nothing else about this situation. She told me she'd been sending me messages on the app and it hurt her feelings that I hardly ever replied, but she understood things were complicated. Or at least she understood well enough until I thought she was someone else.

I said, Messages?

She nodded, chewing at her bamboo straw. The top disintegrated against her lips and I wondered how long it might take for the material to be reborn in her throat. I imagined life growing up her esophagus and sprouting leaves from her vulva. She said, On the app. I messaged you a bunch. It felt nice, getting attention from you.

And you were what? I said. You were jealous of Katrina?

I don't know about jealous, she said, as though I needed a reminder not to flatter myself. But it woke me up to the fact that you make yourself open to other people more than me.

Sure, I said. Of course I do. Emma gave me a look that suggested my use of *of course* was overstated. I shrugged and she told me she'd heard I was on the chopping block—apparently no one expected me to actually come in, and I couldn't hold that against anyone, as I didn't think I would either—and she felt if she didn't just get this out now, she'd lose her nerve when we went back to our screens.

I said, Ah. I considered her information. I spooned mashed potatoes into my mouth until my container was empty. I began to eat Emma's creamed corn. I unbuttoned my jeans. I told Emma I hadn't known it was her. I was relieved the app would not be the ruin of my relationship with the wives. Why didn't you tell me you already knew? I said. When I told you in the bathroom?

I knew you would have been freaked out, Emma said. I didn't want you to think I was some creep.

Creep for enjoying me? I said. Or what?

Emma studied her untouched food instead of me. You wouldn't believe what I watch when I'm alone, she said. You could have been doing almost anything on the internet, and I would have found it.

Because you miss women, I said, and she told me sure, she guessed. I prodded her for more: She missed women, didn't she? She was unhappy with that man of hers? She gave me a funny look and told me she didn't really think about men anymore. Men other than your boyfriend, I said, and she informed me they broke up.

So you're hoping you'll get with me now, I said, and she laughed at me.

Sure, she said. That's why I arranged such a nice date for us. I remembered the time in the bathroom, with her commenting on my feet. Her constant hovering. I wanted to press the corn beneath her eyelids and hold her face in my hands. I wanted to sit on her face. I wanted to piss in her ex-boyfriend's bed. I asked her what she wanted, why she was with me instead of in the office. Behind us, a couple bickered about how many sides to order: Could they really share one order of baked beans? He didn't want to share; he would only let her have one bite.

I drank her tea and turned on her. I thought of the messages I'd believed were from Katrina, their increasing heat. What would you have done, I said, had I replied to you more explicitly on the app?

In a dropped voice, she informed me she would have done whatever I wanted, her laugh like a homecoming dream. Emma informed me we controlled our own destinies. Come on, she said. Unless you're loyal to your Katrina.

I said, I'm not even loyal to myself. The hot sauce sat easy under my tongue. I wondered if the wives were having sex without me. Emma leaned toward me and I made a show of checking for eavesdroppers, but there were only families and strangers alone in suits. Even that bickering couple had departed; I wondered how many sides they had ordered, if that woman was going to be limited to one spoonful or only a single bean. Would he kill her over two? I wondered. I nodded at Emma to continue and she pointed out I had little to lose. She tilted her head to the bathroom and when I stood, she followed. I wiped the grease on the bottom of my blouse. Some oil lingered and I wondered if it might give Emma an infection. I imagined fitting three fingers up to my top knuckles inside of her, then curving them against her walls. I reminded myself to tell her about the wonders of elderberry. Distantly, I noticed my legs felt absent and my neck damp and cold.

The bathroom was a single stall, unisex, and after Emma stepped in behind me, I locked us in. I thought, Live once! I thought, No biggie! I thought, Maybe she'll smash my head into the wall. All yellow-gold tile, like piss dripped from a plastic bottle. I pressed my face to the wall and breathed low. I noticed I felt as small and unwanted as a welt. I told Emma I was sorry and that I was not feeling very well. I blamed the sandwich I had concocted. There was a lot of butter, I said.

Emma patted my hair uncomfortably. In the mirror, she appeared pale, making her blush and bronzer look ghoulish. When I asked if she was okay, she said she wasn't. You think it's food poisoning already, I said, and she reminded me she hadn't eaten. Right, I said. Right. I hoped I was dying.

Emma asked if I was having second thoughts about having, what she called, a little fun. I said, Of course not. I said, I think I'm going to shit myself. She grimaced, her small face a wide line, and moved toward the door. When I grabbed her by both wrists, she steadied in place but her body felt like a brick. I thought, Not a chance. She did not go for the door handle.

On my knees, the toilet appeared a fresh hope. Cleaner than I anticipated, though I still used the remnants of my self-respect to fold several squares of toilet paper into a pile and placed it against the rim. Then I put my forehead straight on it and tried not to breathe in through my nose. When I told Emma I was actually experiencing a sudden wave of nausea, my voice echoed. Toilet bowls do that, I guess.

From behind me, Emma told me she wasn't good at puke. It's why I could never be a mother, she said, laughing. From the ceiling vents, pop music. I felt as sick as my thoughts and so I wanted to push her, test her, earn the result I felt was inevitable. I vomited thick hunks of food and almost no liquid. The sound was not pleasant, and when it ended, Emma impressed me by calling me a bitch. My jaw ached immediately and I wondered, dully, what I would do if I lost my health insurance. I asked Emma if she would do well in jail.

I can't imagine being in jail, Emma said. She asked if we would be together.

The scenario had not crossed my mind but I told her sure. I said, Do you think you'd stay in jail, Emma? Do you think you'd be very good?

She said, Good? She laughed. I guess I always try to be good. I don't want anyone mad at me.

Right, I said. Well, I'm mad at you. I wasn't sure that I was angry, or rather, I wasn't sure what emotion was behind my sudden rage. I felt a delayed indignation at her casual surveillance of my life. I felt like a joke to her, a game. And, too, I felt disappointed she didn't have her hands out, ready and eager to catch my vomit. If I were with the wives, they'd know what to do. If I couldn't get Emma to love me by being sick, I figured I could get what I wanted by hurting her—I have always been a bad person.

Okay, she said. That sounds like it might be a you problem. I said, What?

She said she didn't understand what exactly was going on. I thought we were going to hook up, she said. I didn't realize you were, like, throwing up? I pitched my voice up high to mock her and asked how she didn't have compassion for me, why she wasn't worried about me dying in here. She told me it seemed I had eaten a little too fast, or something? I told her to speak like an adult and drop the question marks.

You're mean, she said after a long quiet. That's why I wasn't honest with you. You were so nice on the app but I knew it wouldn't last. I informed Emma I thought I was very nice to her, all things considered, and she told me not to patronize her. You think I'm an idiot, she said. It didn't even occur to you that I might have known about you camming at work. I could have ruined your life and you still thought I was stupid.

I don't think you're stupid, I said, though admittedly, I did. I think you're young and I think you don't know yourself. I felt very wise, though of course, I couldn't have explained exactly what I meant even if I were at gunpoint.

Helen, she said. You do a terrible job of washing your feet.

I could only get myself to tell her I was more animal than she understood. I wanted her to mother me, to overcome herself, to mimic the care Catherine and Katrina offered and that I continued to sabotage. I wanted to be worthy in my worst state. I turned from her and vomited into the toilet a second time, rancid and sweet. When I lifted my head, Emma was gone.

26

CATHERINE KNOCKED ON MY DOOR THE day after I received my warning. I was home after a humiliating day in the office, sitting, thinking, keeping my feet to myself. Even Emma ignored me. I hoped it might have been my mother at my door, that she might have pursued me in her new freedom, but it was only Catherine's frown I discovered on the other side of my door. I hoped she would notice that I was wearing Katrina's mother's sweater and pants, but she ignored them both and stepped inside without waiting for an invitation. She removed her scarves and told me Katrina was working the closing shift at the shoe store. She's worried, Helen, she said.

I said I was sorry. I asked if she wanted yogurt. I have key lime, I said. And lemon curd.

No, she said. I'm good on that. She straightened her back. I wondered what it might feel like to sleep between the joints of her spine. Small and precarious, like my own life, but warmer, maybe. I have always been tempted by maybes.

Catherine observed the rest of my apartment without comment. I knew this was a slight; her breeding and manners should have kicked in to compliment my home, even though it was hideous. I asked her if she'd like a drink. I have an ice machine, I said. When she ignored me, I poured her a glass of water from my filtered pitcher and dropped ice into the cup. The machine made a horrible, humiliating noise.

Catherine did not take a sip. Helen, she said. Jesus Christ.

I said, Sorry. I said, I didn't mean to ghost. If I were smarter, I could have asked her about her life. If I were less self-involved, I might have asked about her course load. If I hated myself enough, the universe might let me off the hook for Catherine's anger. I closed my eyes and thought bad things about myself: I was silly, stupid, girlish, impossible, a liar, a bore, a death-bringer, a happiness risk, a harpy. When Catherine said my name slowly, I knew my efforts did not work.

I tugged at Katrina's mother's sweater. Catherine put her hands on the top as well. I watched her thumb and pointer finger rub the hem. Catherine kneeled before me and put her face to the fabric, then let her weight come forward, and rested against my stomach. I realized she was crying.

I said I was sorry with a great forced cough. My voice was meager and I hoped Catherine would notice, that she would have mercy on my stupid self. I couldn't imagine telling her about Emma, about my job, but I also wanted to release it, to pour the truth out of myself. I wanted to feel ever more humiliated, more terrible, to anger her even more. I said, Should we get to the couch? I gestured behind me, though she, of course, had seen it from the doorway already. My home allowed little space for hiding. I added, Please.

You look hunted, Catherine said. Your face is all terror and confusion.

Hunted, I repeated. But I've always come to you.

I know, she said. I know. On the couch, she told me she was going to Vermont. We'll be there three months, she said. I imagined red paint and a white porch. I imagined them fisting in a rocking chair out front. I gave myself the most glorious punishments.

I cleared my throat as though absolving phlegm and she put her head in my lap, skull heavy. I sat back against the couch but did not relax my shoulders or my chest. I asked, Did you tell Katrina? I smoothed her hair flat against her head.

Obviously I told Katrina, she said. The skin beneath her eyes was lilac. I wanted to sleep inside of it and wondered what was keeping her up at night; of course, I hoped it was me. The point is, Helen, I've been trying to tell you, and you haven't been around.

Sorry, I said, wondering just how much Catherine would control my life if I let her. When do you leave?

Would they stomach food without me? Sure, I thought. Certainly. She had to say *two weeks* twice for me to register her words.

So we'll have most of spring, I said, and we'll have the summer. She would miss my birthday, I thought, and the worst of Boston's winter; nothing good came in February or March, unless you were newly enough in love to brave windchill for sex and confident enough to believe you'd be offered the chance to spend the night, if not the weekend. And they'd be free of me, I reasoned.

We don't intend to come back here at all, Catherine said. We'll just live in Vermont for three months and think of it like an extended vacation. Maybe foster some chickens.

Chickens, I said. Is that a conflict of interest? Are they rescue chickens? I imagined Catherine and Katrina in tall rainboots mucking through bird shit. Saving farm-factory animals would require black face masks with holes around the eyes. Would they name them after me. One Helen after another. Squawking and unable to fly. Terrified beasts with thin bones.

Catherine sighed. She said, That part is a work in progress. But now, with you, well. She kept her eyes closed. Katrina will want you to visit us. And instead of you renting a car back and forth, or any of us freezing on the train, maybe come up one weekend and see if you like it, and if you do . . .

If I do? I thought, She wants me. Or she wanted me. My bladder felt warm and narrow. I told her I technically didn't make my own schedule; there are days I might have to come in. I wanted to see how badly she wanted me with them, how much she would negotiate, how deeply she would plead. I thought Catherine spent a lot of time trying to break me and hoped I could break her in return.

So quit, she said. I tensed, watching her face, and she rolled her eyes. Just be an adult, Helen, she said. Jesus Christ. Request a few weeks off, or something? I don't know. Maybe come to us in March and stay the month, and we'd come back to Massachusetts together.

I didn't expect you to offer, I said. I didn't think you'd come here. I wanted women to love me, certainly. The wives especially. And I wanted to remain disposable, forgettable too. The wives imagining me in their future excited and un-nerved me. I told Catherine as much, and poorly; I rambled, saying I thought I'd be easy to leave in Massachusetts, easy to delete, easy to leave alone at home. Catherine was not pleased at my vulnerability and I regretted my bravery immediately.

Right, Catherine said. Because I seem like the kind of person who just shrugs women off. I seem that flippant to you? I know Katrina doesn't seem that way.

I said no, she did not seem that way. I finally told her I got a warning at my job. Catherine kept her face neutral and when I was crying, she asked what was the matter—was I worried about rent or my grandmother's nursing home or what. Instead of being honest about my tears, I talked about Emma.

You feel violated, she said. Betrayed by her.

Well, I said. No. She said, What is it then? and I said I felt unchosen, hurt.

Hurt, she said. You wanted to matter.

Yes, I said, surprised at how well Catherine understood me.

You wanted this girl to choose you, she said, and when I nodded, she told me to get her some aspirin. I got it, but I was being unfair, see, asking her to understand things I didn't understand myself.

When I returned from the bathroom with a bottle, she sipped her water and swallowed two pills. I perched beside her on the floor. I asked her to tell me about the place they would rent in Vermont, to describe the face of the building, to name the street, and surprising me, she did. She even told me the house number. She described herself as picky, and terrified of moving the two of them all the way there only to crack and not get a bit of writing done. I told her that sounded like a lot of pressure and she told me it would help if I came.

I said, Really?

She said, Really. She told me she knew I was a mess, that clearly I did not care to keep my home or anything much clean, but would I vacuum and dust their place if they supported me? I laughed until I realized she wasn't.

Are you asking me to be your maid? I said. Or something?

No, she said. Not that word.

You can sublet this place, she said. Save some money. I'll be busy and inattentive, so you can keep Katrina company and take care of things.

I said, What things? I thought about the aforementioned chickens and imagined one of them getting sick, really sick, and me having to administer medicine, having to drive to the clinic, having to demand help from an overworked nurse who did not quite believe the severity of the situation. I was thrilled at the suggestion, understand, and my own eagerness frightened me.

Catherine said I could do some cooking, run some errands, and give her some massages. Couples do it all the time, she said. We could write up a contract, to make you feel safer. She spoke quickly and confidently.

I told Catherine I didn't think I could do it. She asked what was stopping me, if it was those women always messaging me or Emma, if I was hoping things would work out with her. I told her of course not, none of those women, and certainly not Emma, but she had her head stuck on it, and I couldn't blame her; Emma Emma Emma she was saying, all the while pacing circles. I was thinking I had never wanted Emma, not really; her refusal of me, her making me insignificant was not the real hurt, but a hurt that was easier to digest. It was the wives I wanted, and I didn't yet know when to stop testing them, to see them as they were. I told Catherine I was sorry and she ignored me.

I can't lose my job, I said. I fucked around too much never coming into the office.

Don't make this about how forlorn you are, she said. I just presented you with an option you're refusing in spite of the terrible, terrible decisions you make all the time.

Terrible like what? I said. Like going out with you? I wasn't serious; I was testing, testing. I was waiting for her to slam me into my refrigerator. Instead, her voice stayed the same—in tone and in volume—and she said it didn't matter.

What doesn't matter? I said.

You, she said.

I was getting the slam I really wanted, or close to it— confirmation I was meaningless, dismissible, impermanent. I was crying and I was feeling happy. Why don't I matter? I said.

Catherine looked at her feet and I wondered if she was feeling sorry for hurting me, if she was confused about what was real or what wasn't. No, that's me—I'm still confused about what's lived and what's only wanted. We'll bring someone else, she said. Easy. I asked how they would have time, what with all of their requirements, and she told me no, no, I wasn't going to get away with flipping things; I was the one with the little rules and guidelines. Besides, she said. The search is over.

Really, I said. What's her name?

Not your business, she said, and I rolled my eyes, and she told me she didn't want to tell me because I was crazy. I repeated her, really feeling high and mighty, until she looked at my body a long moment and smirked.

What? I said. She's super hot or something?

Catherine faced away from me and spoke while looking toward my window. I wondered if she saw the little boy's ghost. She told me to just forget it, to forget the whole stupid thing, knowing the two of them at all, and I told her that wasn't fair, she was going too far, and she said she wasn't concerned with fairness.

I'm sorry I made you jealous, I said. But you don't need to lie.

Catherine looked up with fresh anger. I'm not lying, she said.

Okay, I said, wondering finally if she was really playing a game with me, if I was supposed to go along with it. I was too amped to let myself feel a single emotion, to process at all what it would mean if they were actually dating some hotter bitch. Tell me about her, then.

Really smart, Catherine said. Sweet and a hard worker. I managed to look unimpressed because Catherine went on, dropping adjectives I wasn't registering but had the effect of *caring* and *reliable* and *trustworthy*, someone who *signed up for morning Pilates* and actually went, they went to *farmer's markets on Sunday mornings* for carrots and potatoes. I was trying to make myself appear as smug as possible, hoping the game was nearly over so we could get back onto the couch and scratch each other's faces, but she brought me back to the present when she said the woman's name was Amy and she had an amazing rack.

Amy, I said. I was thinking of the Amy I'd grown up with, the one who'd found my grandmother. The one I'd ghosted. There had to be a lot of lesbian Amys in Massachusetts, even ones who were nice and had nice breasts. Catherine went on to say they'd been deciding between us, comparing the two, and she had been dumb to make me an offer when we could all see where this was going. Catherine's eyes started to water and I moved toward her for an embrace, really wondering if this Amy was my Amy, but Catherine leapt backward.

She said, We've known you what, a month?

We both knew the precise day but I couldn't bring myself to correct her. I shrugged and tried to present myself as a woman who had other options. I'm playing, I was thinking. See?

I don't know, I said. I guess around the time I started seeing Emma?

Catherine wilted and we both felt it. Seeing, she said, and I nodded. I expected she'd ask questions, demand proof, sit me down and force information out of me. I would lie and lie and lie until she showed me how to earn her forgiveness. I would hurt her and then reassure her that she needn't feel that kind of pain again. I howled a dirty, throaty noise as Catherine walked to the door. I heard her, sort of—she was telling me to stop being so loud, stop being so much all of the damn time, why couldn't I ever control myself? She was calling me stupid and mean and a waste. When she had the front door open, I forced coughs from myself, hoping to soften and manipulate her. I was wondering how likely I would be to survive if I threw myself in front of Catherine's car.

Well, Catherine said. Bye.

I said, I don't feel well. I coughed loudly, kept my eyes open, on Catherine's hands, hoping she would pull magic from her purse. Care so much you can't help it, I was thinking. Show me exactly how much you're willing to take—that's the sort of charade I was working with. Foolish, foolish. Syrup, I said. Please?

I wish I could, she said. But you've messed it all up, Helen, by making me really angry.

I said, I'm even out of my cough syrup.

Frowning, she said, Good.

I said, I'm trying to be better. I motioned to lift my top but she held up a hand and I froze, belly out and heaving.

Catherine said, Don't, and moved to leave me. Unable to process the hurt of being left, despite having pushed for just that, I grabbed her from behind, hands closer to claws than flesh. She reared back, her body statued to marble. She must have heard me hit the floor but she did not turn.

When I picked myself off my floor, she was gone, and I headed right to my medicine cabinet, eager to find it was reliably as full as ever.

27

THE DAY AFTER CATHERINE LEFT ME, Amy replied to my twelve consecutive texts with a thumbs-up emoji. She agreed to meet me at our old spot in the city, a bar frequented by undergraduates from a college neither of us attended. I needed an adrenaline rush to replace the hurt of being left and hoped the familiarity of our spot might help move things along. I wanted to hook up with Amy again because I wanted to hate myself more. And I wanted to know if she really knew the wives. And still, I was only myself, so when Amy arrived outside the place at the tail end of happy hour, I kept studying the slush on the street, pretending not to notice her.

She said, Hey. Amy has always been patient with me.

I said, Oh! Hey. I told myself she would look different, feel different, if she was actually seeing the wives. But before me, she was the same as always. I wondered if she was still going to barre (Or was it Pilates? I was thinking, Was she their Amy?), if she had that longness to her torso, an extension of bone supporting organs recognized as vital. Sex was easy before she found my grandmother—she only knew what everyone in town knew: addicts dead brother heat always being shut off. Her seeing my grandmother's indignity, smelling the rot, being the person who opened the front door—that was too much.

What really kept me from Amy was that I did not want to suffer through steady comfort. I thought someone like Amy would never hit me again, would never call me names, would never be honest with me if they knew all there was to know. Only when I met the wives, when I experienced their own strangeness, their own desire to push and push and push me, did I feel some hope.

I told Amy none of my thoughts and we ordered food without consulting each other; I got the black-bean burger with cheddar cheese—it was a bar for students, but nowhere in Cambridge operates without offering at least one vegetarian sandwich—and a gingerbread beer. Amy got a Reuben and something dark with a thin layer of foam. Amy withdrew almost as soon as the waitress left with our orders; it was at that moment I picked up an unease about her. Amy prided herself on staying smooth but I felt a bruised air in the way she folded down her shoulders. I knew my drop from her life must have hurt her and I did not want to talk about it so I put a hand on her thigh beneath the table. She kicked her leg up and told me to give it a rest.

So, she said once my hands were both above the table. You dating someone? Or should I say, someones?

Yeah, I said. Catherine and Katrina's hurt faces appeared in the wood wall panels and the wood chairs and Amy's chambray shirt. I told Amy, We're good! I sensed a skepticism in her silence and immediately added they'd invited me to move to Vermont. She nodded but stayed quiet. I asked if she was still on the sites.

Nah, she said. We're not doing the open thing anymore.

This reveal was an invitation to talk about her life, I figured, or at least a signal to me that a hookup wasn't going to happen, but I was still fixated on my Amy being the wives' Amy. You haven't gotten to know any married couples? I said.

Amy pushed her hair behind her ears, then untucked it, a habit I recognized from when we used to get drunk at that bar together and I'd ask her to point out which women she'd been talking to while I was pissing. I mean, she said. What?

Like a dancer, I said. Or a former dancer. Or a professor?

Girl, she said. Are you high?

Oh, I said, thinking of the two sleeping aids I'd taken while on the T. Nope!

Great, she said. She thumbed her pint glass and mentioned her girlfriend was waiting at home for her and I nodded to make it clear I got her point; I wasn't going to humiliate either of us by offering to go down on her in the bathroom. Her beer was taller than mine and wider. I mimicked her gesture, then stopped and waited for her to drink. She did, and I did too. I looked at her breasts to see if they were objectively big or if it was only a matter of comparison to mine and she waved her hand in front of her chest.

I can see you, she said. You little perv.

I said, Sorry, and didn't mean it.

She said, What's up? I looked behind her and took in the drinkers. Mostly women, a few men. Beanies and plaid scarves and hoodies from a number of women's colleges outside of the city. No one wore Harvard memorabilia—I suspect because most people were graduate students or postdocs. None of these people were my parents, of course, who were, of course, the people I was actually looking for. I told her I was feeling all fucked up.

Right, Amy said. The waitress brought our food; we both commented that it was fast, and she said we were the only people who ordered something other than fries and onion rings, and I said, Cool, cool. I wiped my palms on my jeans and grabbed my burger. Amy gave me a nod and I bit; I tasted nothing beyond the burn.

So you're feeling bad, Amy said. About what exactly? She was talking with her mouth full, which surprised me; I almost told her she didn't need to work to make herself unattractive, I got her rejection loud and clear, but didn't want her to hit me so early in the night.

You know, I said.

Humor me, she said. Be a big girl.

I wanted us to finally talk, I said. I spoke slowly and dropped eye contact; she surprised me by putting two fingers beneath my chin and moving my face back up. She wasn't smiling.

About, she said.

The day, I said. I've read the reports already. I just want closure, you know?

Amy did not grab her sandwich but did return to her beer. She'd be finished with her drink long before me. I wondered if she would outpace me two to one. She said I was more delusional than she realized and I asked her what she meant and she told me I must be fucking stupid to try to get sympathy from her talking about closure.

Oh, I said. Right. I pivoted. I wanted her to get angrier to enhance my shame. I repeated my closure explanation. I thought, Suck my eyes from my skull. I thought, Stomp on my foot. Amy was still Amy, and only said, If you hadn't ghosted me when I was, you know, traumatized, we might have talked about this at the time.

I slid some fries between my remaining bun and cheese. The burger was already thick and difficult to eat. I needed a challenge, a focal point for pressure and success. There, I thought, mashing the fries down into the butter lettuce and ketchup. Perfect. At her silence, I stared at the top bun and added that I was sorry for going off the map. She smacked the burger from my hands with a flat palm. It landed on my plate, though I wished it had been my lap; Amy was not a woman who would want to destroy me. The table beside us quieted.

Having you know was humiliating, I admitted for the first time. I'm glad you found her, obviously. You basically saved her life. But I didn't know how to see you again without thinking of her, and of my parents, and I just didn't know how to tell you in a way you wouldn't argue with, I added, my voice a mumble. Amy nodded her understanding, or at least, signaling that she heard me, and I tried to tell myself I was being good, being brave, being honest, that Amy too deserved some closure. It was not her fault she was hooking up with me for a couple of months, no strings, just fun, and that we happened to grow up together, not close emotionally, but spatially, and she probably thought she was doing a good thing, stopping in on my grandmother.

Right after Amy found my grandmother, within an hour, as far as I knew, she called me and told me the basics. She had been crying and telling me it was a fluke, just a hunch to go and surprise her. She brought over a stack of thick blankets her mother crocheted, just a little extra love to the family whose heat was always getting turned off. The door was unlocked. That's all I really remembered from the call: the blankets, the good intentions. I ghosted her after that, and in the bar, I wanted answers. I still believed she was the only person who could give them to me.

I told her what I wanted to know: Did Amy hear my grandmother calling from the living room? Did she say, Who is it? Did she say, Please, come on in! Did she say, Help? Did Amy worry she seemed suspicious when she called the police? Performing an unofficial wellness check on a neighbor her parents mentioned they hadn't seen in, hell, a couple of months, not even on the front porch, getting in good sea air? My grandmother had lived in that house since just after she was married at twenty years old. Neighbors knew she liked her sea air. After Amy made the call, I assumed she waited at the front door for the police, afraid of staying near my grandmother, not knowing where to focus her eyes on a naked old woman covered in filth. Was there dread in the officers' eyes already, I wanted to know. Did the horror hit on the front steps or in the doorway. Did they make it down the hallway, carpet over wood, before they thought, Oh, no. Oh, Jesus

Christ. Or was it when they rounded the corner and saw my grandmother on the floor—she'd fallen from the chair she'd been placed in by one or both of my parents—clutching Amy's coat and scarf over her nudity, fingers sagging at the collar, the blankets in a neat stack beside her. Was that when the moment became a memory.

I take it she doesn't remember? Amy cut the crust off her Reuben as she asked. Meticulous and measured with her steak knife. Did she do this in school? No crust on her peanut butter and jelly? When we were sleeping together, our only meals were sips of my cough syrup (Amy was never perfect either) and honey buns from the gas station. No knives, no forks, no crusts.

No, I said. A familiar noise sounded and I glanced down at my phone, puzzled; I kept my app notifications on silent. Amy checked hers and smiled.

Didn't you say you guys aren't doing the open thing? I asked. She rolled her eyes and told me okay, they were doing it, but it wasn't going to include me. I rolled my eyes back and she gave me a slow clap. I bowed and she snapped her fingers against the crown of my head.

Anyway, she said. Maybe your grandmother doesn't want to burden you with it. It's a gift, not knowing.

I don't know about that, I said. The music, a folksy man-and-woman duet, got louder. I got quieter and Amy and I leaned into each other. I smelled acid on her breath. She was so ill, I said. She couldn't walk on her own. You remember that, don't you? The doctors said she fell, she fucked up something in her hip. They found the evidence in her bones. I did not say she must have been in pain for a long time, the single bottle of Tylenol empty beside her, who knows for how long.

Amy told me no one told her what the doctors said and I admitted that made sense. She held my thigh under the table and I pressed into her palm until she withdrew. She said, You ask your parents about it?

I said I didn't. Amy cracked her knuckles inside one palm then the other. The crunch soothed us both. You don't keep in touch? While they're . . . away.

No, I said. We do. Sort of. She looked at me funny and I talked about my father's calls. I told her about my father's request. I admitted I bailed on him and she gave me a neutral nod.

Amy asked if he flipped. I told her yes and she nodded, probably remembering him and his reputation, and said, And your mother?

She's out now, I said. My dad told me she got on probation when he was flipping his shit. Amy whistled and I could not read if she was happy for my mother or disgusted.

She was quiet for a long minute, thumbed her fries, and told me that sounded very difficult. I pushed past her graceful attempt to end the conversation and said, Did you ever run into my parents before it happened? When you were visiting home?

I would have told you if I talked to your parents, she said. I don't hide things.

But you saw them, I said. She admitted yes, she'd seen them around, a couple of weeks before she knocked on my grandmother's door.

I said it was nice she saw her parents so often and she told me, yeah, she saw them most weekends. I wondered what that might be like: I remembered her parent's house from birthday parties in elementary school, the kind where the whole class was invited. Modest, but clean, and filled with knickknacks and lit candles. I was shocked at the neat arrangement of family photos and school pictures on the refrigerator. Our fridge was covered in yellowed bills. I asked Amy what my mom and dad had looked like.

Your mom looked pretty out of it, Amy said. Holding herself upright and all, but had that glassy look. Moving in molasses. And your dad was up and all over the place, wandering the sidewalks. He had all of her energy, it looked like.

The waitress came by and checked on us; we told her it was wonderful, so great, but she was already surveying the next table, the next people she had to keep a smile for. As she passed us, Amy said people in town gossiped. When word got around about your grandma going to the hospital, she said, and the house being empty and all, people talked.

They're still talking, I said.

Yeah, she said. Some. Amy gave me the gift I longed for. I was present and I was not. I broke my burger into small pieces and put each one into my mouth. I tore at the patty with my index fingers. I split my fries like bones. Amy nudged her plate toward me and I peeled some of the cheese and sauerkraut from her sandwich and ate that, also with my fingers. Amy did not detail the smell, and so I imagined every smell: blood feces urine sweat fear tears anticipation dry mouth breath in my own cupped hand. Her voice was serious when she told me my grandmother had been speaking when she entered. Amy had assumed someone else was home, or that she was on the phone, though my grandmother's voice sounded weak and distorted. She kept asking for her children to come back, Amy said. She said they'd just left.

When I threw up outside, Amy grabbed me by the belly and kept me upright. Hey, she said. Hey.

We had no chemistry, no heat. Gone, from my own doing. I was not sure how we would move forward, or how I had existed at all, with her knowing what she knew.

When my vomit really started, smokers stepped to the end of the block, exposing themselves to stronger wind. Amy rubbed my back and told me she understood. She did not tell me it was okay, all fine, all good, but that she understood. When I lowered myself to my knees, she stooped. From that angle, her nose showed its crooked bend, knocked that way from softball in our second or third year of high school. When I looked up from my vomit, all dark in white snow, her nose was not wrinkled.

I'm sorry I hurt you, I said. She asked what was so hard about saying those words, why the months of silence, and I told her I thought she was over it.

She said, Over it?

I get it now, I said. I just didn't think you cared.

I'm taking you home, she said. There's no way I'm dropping you off somewhere else tonight. I refused to leave well enough alone and told her I didn't think she would have missed me and she was seeing someone now, wasn't she? Probably someone who wasn't a fuckup. Amy pushed me a little and I swayed myself back into her chest. Not everyone is as self-centered as you, Helen, she said, and I informed her I hated myself, and she said that had nothing to do with my inability to accept accountability. She told me she gets why I do the push-and-pull bullshit but that I don't get to tell myself the person being dragged around doesn't give a shit.

Look at yourself, Amy said. You really think anyone would show up for you if they didn't care? I told her I thought exactly that, though I couldn't articulate why—my brain was spinning from the beer and sleep aids and, of course, I was embarrassed at her accurate read of me. She told me to cut the drama and let her take me home.

I put my head on her shoulder and said on one condition. I was feeling her breasts through both of our big coats and sweaters and came to the unhappy conclusion that they were objectively large and better than mine. She said, Jesus Christ, I'm not kissing you. I said I knew. She said, What, then?

Do you know the wives? I said. Catherine and Katrina.

She appeared to think about it and told me no, she didn't. Do *you* know these wives?

I don't know, I said, feeling uncharacteristically honest.

Is this who you want to talk about right now? she said. Or what? I told her it wasn't, not really, I was looking for new monsters again. So what is it? she said. What do you want from me?

Were my parents happy? I said. When you saw them.

No, she said. They looked really, really sad. I told her I

needed to know more, to know everything; I wanted to punish myself, yes, that's what I told myself outside the bar, with
Amy holding me up. Only later would I admit I wanted to
know enough to be free of the pain I projected onto myself.

On the sidewalk, Amy only said we both knew who I had
to talk to and I managed to admit I knew just where to go.
Almost.

28

THE RENTAL CATHERINE DESCRIBED looked like all the other houses in the neighborhood. Rectangular building with tall, thin windows, several stories high, and none held my father. I wanted our faces to appear side by side. To people passing us on the sidewalk we'd appear peculiar: an older man and a younger woman eating and scowling and looking straight outside instead of at each other. But my father and I would be fine watching snow accumulate on trees. If passersby noticed the ghost behind us, so be it. I was ready to be seen.

After seeing Amy, I called the wives over and over, hysterical and desperate. They pointedly told me not to come; they'd see me when they got home from Vermont, after they had time to think. Within hours of being told to stay in and take care of myself—to go easy on my syrup—I spent sixteen dollars on my bus ticket and ate french fries in South Station, rabid in my wanting. In the station, I considered turning to Emma, to get the quick fix of superficial agony, but I wanted a deeper pain, a bigger finish.

After a nine-hour ride I walked from the Burlington bus

station to their rental. I knew I would miss work and would not have an excuse; I imagined doctoring a note but decided against it. All in, I was telling myself. Or what is the point. The whole journey I thought CKCKCKCKCKCK and circled the house number in my mind. And now, somehow, it stood before me.

On the porch, I saw a woman smoking. Wrapped in a long white robe, with a white towel wrapped around her head and a bend in the middle of her nose, she reminded me so much of Catherine. I wondered if she might be the other woman they were seeing. Not Amy, surely even in my state I knew I would recognize her, but Amy's replacement, I told myself— the thought of both of us being disposable to the wives made me feel a little better.

I walked toward the house, still on the sidewalk, and the woman turned toward me. She said, Helen?

I said, Catherine? I realized my bladder was very full. I stepped my legs closer together and blinked up at her. My throat no longer felt hot but numb and I understood this shift as a kind of gift, a leaning toward invincibility.

Catherine repeated my name. I advanced and noticed she was in house slippers I had never seen before. She said, I thought you were a madwoman.

I told her I guessed I was a madwoman. She did not laugh. I saw you from down the block, I said, but I didn't recognize you with the cigarette. I thought of Katrina smoking and wondered if Catherine knew. The small secret made me happy.

I smoke once in a while, she said flatly. Helen, are you going to explain why you're here? It's barely six in the morning.

I know, I said. I wanted to kill some time before calling you. I was afraid I'd wake you up. I was thinking, You and your other girlfriend, but held it in.

You came to Burlington, Catherine said. For us? Or what? Where are you staying? She looked up and down the street. Did you park around here?

I didn't drive, I said. I took the bus.

She repeated after me. She put out her cigarette. She said, How long did that take? I told her and she said that sounded like a nightmare. I said it wasn't too bad. I told her about a man wearing a gray sweatsuit who resembled my father but wasn't. She asked if we had a nice chat and I said not really, but before he was arrested, he sat next to me. I think he felt comfortable with me, I said. She told me to come inside and take my shoes off at the door.

On the stairs, she whispered, I feel like I'm in high school. Sneaking you in. Catherine pushed a door open and revealed a large bedroom facing the backyard and a small pond. Katrina did not open her eyes until I said her name. Then she blinked with her face against the pillow until Catherine gave her the rundown. The bed was otherwise empty and I was foolish enough to believe my work with the wives was done.

She said, Helen's here? Still she did not lift her head. I sat on a chaise at the end of the bed. Catherine told me to get in and lie down, but change first; I smelled like hell. I stayed sitting while I stripped to my underwear, which was dirty, as I had not changed since yesterday morning. Catherine waved at me to hurry. When I pulled a clean pair, maroon and high-waisted, from my backpack, she watched me lower myself.

The indignity of stepping into underwear is a special moment to behold. I wanted to thank her, but instead, I got into bed beside Katrina, shy. Catherine dropped onto my other side. Above us, the bed's four posters held a curtain. The wives left it open for our good light.

Katrina pulled my face closer to her own. You're here, she said, giving me the sleepy happiness I desired. Her hair smelled of green apples. In bed, I believed we would not talk about any of it. Katrina's solo drive. Catherine's visit. Either of their secret smoking. My grandmother. Amy. Of course, I was wrong.

You might have called, Catherine said. But you know that already. Tell us why?

I described the conversation with Amy. That sounds like a lot, Katrina said. Do you know if you feel better?

I told her I didn't know. The room, I decided, smelled like gingerbread. I closed my eyes.

Your guilt doesn't make a lot of sense, Katrina said. You were a kid. And when you were grown up, your dad treated you like shit.

I said, What? Katrina told me it wasn't okay, the way he spoke to me, calling me a dyke and a cunt and whatever else. She let me know her parents never spoke to her that way, even when she was a real bitch. I knew I had not told her those things, those accurate, specific things, and moved my mind to figure it out. Had they hacked my email? I never wrote to anyone about my father. Diary? I didn't keep one. I wondered if I had begun talking in my sleep.

Tell me what you know, I said. Katrina gave her wife, who nodded, a look of permission, and then informed me they'd found the statement I typed up for my father in the pocket of my coat. I asked what she was talking about, though I knew precisely what she meant, and even recalled my vague but ultimately minimal anxiety about misplacing that folded piece of paper. Still, I wanted to feel in control, to know all there was to know about these women I could not predict, who would do whatever it took to stay ahead of me, and I wanted to hear them articulate their efforts in a way that felt manageable to me. Katrina hung her wife out to dry, stressing Catherine actually went through my stuff while I was asleep, but admitted she herself read the letter first, then showed her wife. I liked imagining them pulling the paper between them, fighting over who would know me first.

Why did you write the statement? Catherine cut in. Second thoughts?

I admitted I wanted to want my father to get out. I'm not a monster, I said. I know he's living in a shithole. I considered my unhappy truth: I could forgive my father of his latent homophobia, and I had. I could bear to send empathy to my parents but could not act on it, not without telling my own body goodbye. I was going to tell the wives, but realized their eyes were on each other and not on me. So I pulled back and wondered aloud how I didn't notice the missing statement sooner. I'm always reaching into that pocket for my medicine, I said.

You walk through the world with your elbows in front of your face, Helen, Katrina said. I rolled my eyes and Catherine asked what would make me change my mind about my father and I told her nothing.

I can't do this if I don't move on from it, I said. By *this* I

meant be with them, sure, and hold a job, and wash my armpits, and smile at waiters, and orgasm. In that Vermont rental,
feeling sicker whenever I remembered I had a body, I asked if
we could talk about something else, something lighter. Catherine filled her wife in on the conversation we'd had in my
apartment, about her offering for me to stay with them. I wondered, briefly, what the hell went on in these women's minds:
How could she possibly feel that was the right time? And
yet I sat transfixed by Katrina as she morphed her eyebrows
to interested, and when Catherine was done, I had learned
nothing new except that Katrina did not always remove her
mascara before sleep. The crust around her eyes softened and
frightened me: What else didn't I know about these women?
I waited for Katrina to speak and after I nudged her with my
foot below the blanket, her skin somehow cold, she asked me
how I was feeling. Did I have any questions?

I said, Questions? I told her of course I had questions. I
asked if they'd lived with a partner before and Katrina looked
over my head at her wife.

We haven't, Catherine said. But we have thought about it,
which is I think what you're actually asking. I demanded to
know who the woman was and Catherine told me I already
knew: the woman with the scotch.

I said, The woman in the photo. The mess? I asked how
long they'd been seeing her and they said about two months.
They suggested a trial period, and she was happy to move right
in, eager to get away from three roommates, but she stayed
less than a week. I asked why and Katrina said the depth of
the woman's drinking, previously a secret, spooked her.

Why don't you wait longer? I said. You barely know me.

We like a rush, Katrina said. In a loud whisper, she added, Especially Catherine—she likes the way you move, like you're always skirting a villain you made up in your own head. Her wife reached above me and smacked Katrina on the mouth, playful. I hoped Catherine would hit me too and when she didn't, I said I would need to get a new job, I couldn't just play house forever. I asked them how sustainable they thought this plan could be, if they'd really considered all the possible disasters. Catherine told me I could worry about whatever I wanted, but they weren't the ones subsisting on cough syrup and fructose.

It's not a silly worry, I said. It's not like Katrina sells shoes for fun, you know? Really, I was worried about them kicking me out as quickly as they'd let me in. Beneath the blanket, I reached for both of their hands and they let me take them though neither one squeezed.

I don't work for fun, Katrina said. But my family does help. Quieter, as though embarrassed, she added she wouldn't work in Vermont.

I repeated, Family? I thought of her mother and that house in Maine. It did not seem so grand to me, so extravagant that Katrina would be able to stumble through adulthood with a trust fund. She said that her parents, and Catherine's too, gave them the down payment for their home. That helps a lot, with our budget, she added, and I said I would imagine so. Katrina added that the cost of their monthly payment was actually so much less than rent and I thought about how much I spent every month to live in a place with one good window. I imagined elbowing her in the teeth.

Great, I said. The three of us stayed in bed. I tucked my face beneath the top sheet and coughed. The sound from my throat was thick and glossy. Catherine said that didn't sound good, and Katrina agreed, saying I felt a little warm to the touch. When Catherine said she'd dig up the thermometer from her purse, I felt chosen. I asked how long they'd been thinking about asking me to move in with them, or if it came up because of the move.

Since the cafe, Katrina said. Remember, with the pancakes? She spoke as though our first date wasn't barely a month prior. I laughed, flattered, and she laughed a little too. I told her to be serious, I really wanted to know, and she said she was telling the truth. We think about it with every woman we go out with, she said. We keep it in mind.

I asked what made me a good choice.

Catherine returned with the thermometer and told me to open my mouth. I obeyed and Katrina explained they liked that I didn't make an effort, that they got to see me precisely as I was. It's exhausting when women pretend to be someone else, she said. But you didn't even brush all of your hair for the cafe, remember? They laughed then and I laughed too, the thermometer still in my mouth, until Catherine tapped my nose, firm and happy.

Catherine told me she was glad I didn't ask the obvious: Why hadn't they told me when we first met? I nodded, knowing that such transparency on their part would have foiled the game. I asked if they had thought of ruining me, outing me at work as a cammer. Catherine asked if I hadn't gotten my way and I asked her if she meant to be ruined and she told me, No, to be caught camming. Then she told me to check my phone.

Your screen keeps lighting up, she said. The number isn't saved. After the thermometer beeped, she tugged it from my mouth without warning and said I seemed more than a little sick. Check your phone, she said. Then you're resting.

Yes, I said. Sure. I had two calls from the prison from the night before, and seven missed calls from my father's attorney from earlier that morning. Three voicemails, all from the attorney. I wondered if he might be calling to guilt me into submitting a statement all over again. A team effort. My father had few options and his life was filled with indignities. He, too, was human. Hadn't I won in the ways that mattered? I got out of poverty's hell and he wanted out of a worse one. In bed with Katrina, I reminded myself I was not a good person. I deleted the voicemails without listening.

Back beside us in bed, Catherine said, Tell me you're sorry. I told her I was, thinking she was happy to punish me, happy to regain some control after her wife had revealed their playing hand. Happy, too, to know that real sickness did not inhibit our fun. She said, No. She said, Say it like I say it. I told Catherine I was sorry with my voice flatter, fuller, reaching all corners of the vowels. To my own ear, I sounded precocious. I thought, Hit me, hit me. Sweat behind my knees and ears.

Where is your other woman? I said, and the wives looked at each other. I said, Where's Amy?

Amy, Catherine repeated slowly, as though testing syllables in her mouth. Amy.

The one with the boobs, I said. Remember? I was feeling confident they didn't really know my Amy, but confused, too, as to why Catherine had hurt me without any of the delight, without any of the nurturing afterward. I looked to Katrina as I spoke, curious to see if she had any envy or insecurity on her face, but she only looked attentive, as though we were performing for her benefit.

We were lying about that, Catherine said.

You were lying, Katrina said. She smirked at me and informed me that her wife loves to lie. Catherine can't handle rejection, she added. Makes her nuts.

I don't love to lie, Catherine said, using air marks for quotes. Why am I the monster here? I asked them to please not fight and Katrina beamed. I said I understood they wanted to hurt me and regain control. I told Catherine she had done all the right things: made me feel bad, disposable, a failure, and there I was, back to them, a good girl.

But Amy, I said. Why that name?

You mentioned her, Catherine said. At the picnic, remember? I shook my head and she reminded me I'd named her as the ex that had found my grandmother, and it came back to me, my horrible vulnerability. So accustomed I was to blocking out moments of honesty.

We both messed up, I said to the wives. Understand I could not have felt more flattered that Catherine remembered such a detail and had the foresight to use it as a test.

Tell me you love me, Catherine said. I balked, shy-like. She gathered herself up and rose from the floor. Together, we eyed the desk in the study nook of their bedroom: notebooks manilla folders loose-leaf paper pens without caps. I wondered if they'd been working or writing about me or doctoring up a will. At my insolence, Catherine repeated herself and picked up a yellow ruler, offered me the saddest smile. I knew Catherine was too emotional to use her hands on me, what with their cards on the table and no direct yes from me. The ruler, I thought, perfectly placed—Katrina might consider it fate—constituted a peace offering.

Catherine's hits were not gentle but not strong; she was more limp than muscle, more stretched than squeezed. She knelt beside me on the bed, my body still, back flat on the mattress, and Katrina curled on her side to watch after tugging the blanket down to my ankles. Stings blossomed on the tops of my hands and I wondered, vaguely, if the veins were important. My little arm fat swayed when she made her way up toward my shoulders. At my head, Catherine hesitated. I gave her a nod, and she returned it, but hesitated, and so I said, Go ahead.

She said, You first.

I said, What?

Catherine told me no. She said, Use your head. I nodded to prove I was capable of being useful. She said, Tell me you love me. I hesitated and she struck my forehead twice. Two times, I guessed, for making her repeat herself. I mouthed, I love you. She struck the crown of my skull. I mouthed, I love you, again and again, my mouth a dry circle, and she made a show of striking all about me. The room filled with the sound of not thuds but pats, disorienting my reality. How could I feel something so deeply, the drum drum drum of cheap wood against the flesh of me, and hear it only as a whisper, a giggle. I felt Katrina rubbing herself beside me.

At my jugular, Catherine thumped, thumped and I said, I love, love you. My voice a funny admission of ugly hope. I loved the wives, or at least I thought I did; saying the words felt as much a gamble, a test for myself, a test of them, as anything else. I thought of Katrina's talk about one action changing everything, the way minor decisions roll out and out and out. I did not know what might happen if I was lying about love, or if I was being sincere. I hoped I might die either way.

After some time, enough to leave my body reddened but not bruised, I rolled not so much against Catherine as into her. Catherine emitted a groan I could only understand as joy. I heard Katrina orgasm. To Catherine, I said, I never noticed you were left-handed.

She said, I know. With her right hand, she formed a fist and tapped the crown of my head. I raised my skull until our foreheads touched. Her nose, bent in the middle, emitted thick breaths. I stuck my tongue up and trailed the edge of her nostrils, happy to realize she did not trim her nose hairs with any appearance of regularity. Catherine grunted.

I said, I didn't call out of work today.

She said, Mm?

I said, I didn't get any more time off, no leeway. I saw her open her mouth and told her no, it probably wasn't entirely legal, but the point was I quit. I basically turned in my notice, I said, though I didn't really believe it would go down that easy.

She said, Okay.

I said, Okay?

Beside her, Katrina chirped, Okay!

I said, Can I sleep in your bed? I was waiting for them to laugh, to tell me they were so honored I was accepting their offer, that I had taken the plunge, dropped from the ceiling into their world. I was feeling tired too, and warm: Was gas leaking into the room? Had they injected me by way of a small needle into a good amount of fat? I imagined the ruler left handprints at my neck, though that was only wishful thinking. My wives were special but could not create the impossible at every turn.

Catherine said, May you? She knocked me harder on the head. I imagined her knuckles inside of me. I wanted to ask if she was a good fister, and in an effort to build up to the subject, I asked again, May I sleep in your bed? My voice was decidedly sweet. I felt certain then, is what I am getting at. I was thinking, Finally. I was thinking, Here we are. I was thinking, Wow. I was thinking I could not see entirely straight.

The wives said no and after some moments, I dragged myself to a chair and slept until the next morning.

29

CATHERINE INFORMED ME I SOUNDED awful. From my spot on the chair in the corner of their temporary bedroom, I lied and said I felt great. Since my hours on the overnight bus, I continued to feel sicker and sicker, coughing during the night, and hoped they would coddle me. Katrina said if I really felt great, would I mind heating up some water for tea? I looked around the room then, thinking they had an electric kettle set up, and the wives laughed. Downstairs, Katrina said. In the kitchen.

I said, Sure. I asked if they wanted breakfast and they shook their heads no.

That would be too much to ask of you, Catherine said. Choose a lemon tea for yourself, with lots of honey, and don't skimp on the milk—I don't think you'll eat today so you'll want the sustenance. She toweled off her hair as she spoke. If you'd like me to do it instead, she added, just ask.

I'm good, I said, though I needed to curl beneath a blanket and turn my body inside itself. On my lonely journey down the stairs and into the kitchen, I comforted myself with the notion I could drop and die at any given moment. I might split the space between my eyes if I fell forward into the oven. My head might knock the knobs and turn on the gas stove. I would shout to the wives to run from fire. I felt I was a very good person then.

Boiling water was simple and forgettable. I considered adding fresh lemon juice but worried I would cut my hand off slicing one open. A cut to the top of the wrist would not seal the deal, but a taste of adrenaline suggested I could dig into bone and might not be able to stop trying. I wondered, vaguely, if I should tell the wives about my fantasies. I dug through the drawers in hope of a forgotten decongestant but all were empty.

Into a blender, I dropped cubes of ice, spinach, one banana, seven strawberries, a regrettable amount of flaxseed, handfuls of blueberries, a generous amount of white liquid from a clear bottle labeled *almond milk*, and, after poking in the cabinets, dried elderberries. I breathed in through the bag opening and smiled. All was earthy and all was good. I convinced myself they planned to make more syrup and that I would be well soon. I added two handfuls and returned it to its safe place.

When I took the first sips, I felt wonderful, even in my worsening state. I told myself I was doing a great job. The smoothie tasted almost entirely of banana, though I could not understand why. I decided to introduce my concoction to the wives as an immunity booster and split the remainder between two other glasses that I carried close to my chest as I climbed the stairs. I felt sweat beneath my breasts.

When I approached the bed, Catherine eyed the glasses. She said, That's a funny-looking tea, Helen.

I said, Oh. I'd forgotten about the tea. I told her to try the smoothie instead. It's amazing, I said. There's a secret ingredient.

The wives did not ask what the ingredient was, disappointing me. You need the nutrients, Katrina said. It'll help you. She nodded to Catherine, who put her robe on and left, I guessed, to retrieve the abandoned tea. I told Katrina I wanted her to try at least a sip and she said no.

I said, Why? My voice split. I could not handle even the smallest rejection with any degree of grace.

Katrina gave me a noncommittal look. Don't obsess, Helen, she said. I just don't want it. Behind me, Catherine's footsteps on the stairs.

I'll save you some, I offered. I realized I could not expect the wives to forgive me with ease again and again. I told them they looked beautiful and they looked at each other to laugh, excluding me.

She never even made the tea, Catherine said. She tsked in her familiar way, a comfort. I turned from the pair of them and I drank my glass down. Then Katrina's glass. Then, finally, the third. The liquid curdled in my stomach. I felt the wives watch me but they did not speak. The cool felt divine on my throat. Better than a fist. I thought I was being smart, and also vengeful, and, most importantly, winning. If they craved a sip, there would be none left. It occurred to me I had not cleaned the blender or any of my mess. I felt close to dying then, so I crawled not beside Katrina but onto the chair. In my last waking moments, I felt triumphant, victorious. Bright.

In the afternoon, I woke to the realization that my body

had wet itself on the chair. The wives bent over me and informed me they were going for a hike; I hoped they would notice the scent of urine, but if they did, they did not mention it, disappointing me. Catherine simply told me not to do anything foolish while they were gone. I said, Cool! I slept. Sweat came from my forehead neck back breasts and below, the ribspace where heavy flesh meets almost-bone. Ligaments said, Forget it, and let go. Muscles accelerated into fat. To steady myself as I rose, I cupped my own bare breasts. I did not slam the bathroom door behind me but I did think to lock it.

In the bathroom, my brain guided my body: eyes shut colon clenched arms crossed. What else would a body do but hold itself together. Balanced on my knees, I retched onto the toilet. Because I had not thought to lift the lid, my insides splattered across the white top and down the white sides and onto the white floor. In the dark, I guessed my vomit was purple. Lilac, violet, lavender. I lowered my face to the tile and sniffed: sweet like maple syrup boiling beneath concrete. I retched again, this time managing to lift the lid. In the bowl, I believed I saw fresh colors: lemon lime apricot crimson. I ran my tongue along the backs of my teeth and thought, Holy shit. The world appeared small and dark. It occurred to me that the time to call out for help may have passed.

And what help did I want? I felt frightened and loved. I was thinking it had to have been ethylene glycol. The almond milk, I decided, must have been laced with just enough to poison me. Odorless and overly sweet, I wouldn't have realized as I sucked down cup after cup. And the wives refused to have even a sip. Their plan was perfect, and I was a good, happy girl,

minus their absence. I wish they'd whispered instructions—
was I to scream or beg or grovel or wait inside myself. Had
they really hiked or were they down the hallway, listening for
a thump? If I lived, I resolved to tell them we'd need to go over
more ground rules the next time.

I placed my cheek against the rim and closed my eyes. I
wanted to flush the vomit away but could not quite lift either
of my arms. Instead, I rubbed my fingers inside and against my
crevices: armpits arch of feet top of ass crack behind the ears
my nostrils. Palm to my mouth, I smelled myself and wondered what was departing. Before I dropped back into myself,
my body slipping from toilet to tile, I smelled white soap and
menthol, the odor of a boy never ruined by manhood. I felt
very happy then.

I awoke intermittently to a clattering at the door and light
from beneath the frame. I covered my crotch with my hands.
I felt a crusted substance between my thighs and wondered if
it were urine or feces and did not have the energy to check. I
wondered if my grandmother felt similarly the first, second,
third, fourth, fifth time she realized she was sick and alone.
I thought, Jesus Christ. The knob twisting, twisting. Thudding, thudding. Catherine was angry and Katrina sad. No,
Catherine was sad and Katrina angry. From my spot on the
floor, curled into the fetal position with one ear nestled into
the bath mat, I could not discern their voices. I heard my
name, or a word like my name, over and over. When wood
splintered, I noticed I was thirsty. I said, Hello?

Together the wives said, Helen! My eyes were shut but I

believed their faces said, I love you! Or, We did not sign up for this. Or possibly, Perfect.

One turned on the shower while the other took to me with a damp washcloth. Both said, Helen, Helen, Helen. One—Catherine, I believe—called me a stupid, stupid woman. In time, I realized Katrina was the one bathing me, rinsing the same cloth under the faucet, whispering niceties I could not make out. Catherine fiddled with products beneath the sink and called her mother. Katrina informed me you had to cook elderberries before consumption. They're totally poisonous if you have them in a smoothie, she said. There's cyanide in the seeds. She added that I had left a small-scale disaster in the kitchen.

But the milk, I said.

The wives said, What?

The almond milk, I said. I used it in the smoothies.

I didn't mess up the almond milk, Catherine said. I make it all the time. She moved her eyes all around as though she were trying to avoid rolling them. You messed up because you did a stupid thing.

I said, Oh. Katrina told me in a low voice that Catherine was worried I would die, and I tried to ask her if this was part of the game or not, but she shushed me.

Holding the phone away from her ear, Catherine kept her mother on the line and asked Katrina questions about me, like, Does it seem like she threw up any blood? And, How do her pupils look? And, most abhorrent to me: We're positive she's not pregnant, right? Katrina mostly shrugged until eventually suggesting that they really might want to drive me to a clinic. Still naked and half-covered in filth, I held her hand and said, No, no. I would stay a mess, surrounded by vomit and piss, if it meant I had their attention—even if it was less attention than I wanted, I told myself to be grateful, be good, be pure. They were wiping me, after all.

Evening had arrived by the time the wives got me standing in the shower. Catherine monitored the temperature of the water, warm but not too warm, and fretted over whether or not I had a concussion. Katrina started with the soap down at my feet. I'd been bathed by women before, post-sex, with a strong focus on lathering each other's breasts and backs. In this shower, in this rental, with yellow flowers adorning the ceiling, my body understood a queer weakness. When I leaned against Katrina, soaking her T-shirt, she did not remove herself. I smiled into her chest as she soaped and rinsed my vulva. Her fingernails massaged my stubble and I thought, This is it. I thought, Good has arrived. Emma had perhaps awoken me to the inevitable fatigue of my own self-destruction. Fate, I was thinking, telling myself Katrina was right once more about the importance of small things.

I was coming down from my fever and felt unusually secure in my ability to understand myself, and so I told Katrina I had an answer to their question. She asked me to hold off. You're barely coherent, she said. Don't spoil the whole thing by rushing it.

Later, while Katrina rubbed shampoo into my scalp, her nails doing the good work, the work of God even, Catherine stood to the side and asked me questions. She wore the robe she'd smoked in, likely having changed into it after scrubbing dried vomit off the base of the toilet. The window was opened only a crack, and Katrina mentioned that was for the best. So none of us can escape, she said. I knew she meant, So none of us can die that way.

Catherine made the water a little hotter. What's my name? she said. I wondered if my flesh would blister and if they liked to pop skin and monitor the growth of pus. She stood back from the stream, her face obscured by steam, but I saw her open mouth, a smile and a scream, an *o* of pleasure and of shock. I understood anticipation in her round abyss, her wanting me to answer but as always, the question I was hearing was not the right one, not the one she was asking. I hoped she was testing me in the way I needed; I hoped I had her full attention.

I said, Catherine. I did not reach for her or plead or shout. Catherine turned the knob until the water ran cold and I yelped. I could not resist it; my body pimpled over, my nipples perked. I kept my hands at my sides, even looked to Katrina, who was only smiling, and I said, Catherine? I said, Catherine! In the slim shower, I had no escape. Maybe she wanted me to push past them, to force myself out, to save myself—but no, of course that was not it. I dropped to my knees and put my hands on my thighs. I held my face up beneath the water and let it enter my nose and open mouth until I coughed and sputtered and coughed and sputtered. I felt two hands pull me forward and when I opened my eyes, I saw the wives parallel before me, all contentment. What relief in everyone knowing their part.

I told them they knew precisely how to care for me. What

I meant: They knew precisely how to love me. Catherine ignored this and said, How did you meet me? Her smile was all in her voice and so I answered without fear.

I said, The internet. Katrina turned the water back to warm and tugged me upright by the shoulders. She pressed my head under the shower stream and soap gathered on top of my eyes. I wanted to keep them open, to see purification in action, but my eyelids resisted.

Catherine said, Where do you work?

With my face still under the stream, I said, Nowhere. I wondered what it might be like to take a vacation with the wives, a real vacation, with sun and an ocean. I told myself to ask them later if they would hold me beneath a wave. One gripping my wrists, the other my ankles. In my fantasy, I could hear laughter above the waves while being held beneath, though in reality it would likely only be a pulsing in my ears. What bliss in a body moving with resistance.

Catherine and Katrina tugged my head out from beneath the warm water and I opened my eyes in time to watch the wives exchange a look. Catherine said, And why is that?

I said, Because I'm a stupid person. Katrina tugged my hair at the scalp and I rolled my eyes. I said, And because men ruin all good things. The wives nodded and Catherine removed her robe. She told Katrina I could wear it when she was done with me and offered no explanation for her nude departure.

I really thought you were dead, Katrina said after Catherine closed the door.

I was curious about what the scene looked like, as I have always wanted to observe from outside of myself. How nice to watch myself talk to people from above, nestled into the corner of a ceiling or balanced on the top of a window frame. What a glory to see myself make horrible, feckless decisions in the face of good women. How did you feel? I asked Katrina instead. When you thought I was dead.

I didn't feel anything, Katrina said. I think I was in shock.

I told her I could understand that numbness. Catherine, she added, was having a conniption. She just kept saying, Helen's dead, over and over, like an incantation.

I asked if she comforted her wife and Katrina shook her head. You had to be there, she said. Well. You had to be awake.

As she turned off the faucet, I said, I really thought you'd poisoned me. I flapped my body back and forth, hair flinging like a dog's, and Katrina withstood the sprays. She asked if I was disappointed and I admitted I was and she was quiet for a while before she told me they couldn't have that sort of fun with me if they didn't think I was stable, if I wasn't at least on their level. It ruins the rush if you're out of our control, she said, and we stayed quiet until I nodded my assent. I told Katrina I wanted to know what was up with her wife; I thought I understood what she wanted to hear, how to play her game, but I'd seen an anger, a heat I couldn't recognize as solely good or bad. I wanted, mind you, to learn this anger so I could summon close to it when desired.

Holding the robe up for my arms, Katrina said, Catherine used to think she wanted a woman that was easy to control, you know, simple. Then she pulled the robe back from me, leaving me naked and wet and happy, and said, But she came around to the thrill, the wild you bring. I asked her why the anger, then, if she had come around. I worried Catherine would reject me now, especially since I had warmed to the idea of living with them.

I added, I'm only being the way I know how to be.

Katrina told me none of us are happy with what we want, not all of the time. She used her pointer finger to tug my eyelids down and I felt in my new darkness a relief and a foreboding.

30

THE WIVES LET ME STIR TOGETHER the goat cheese, elderberries simmered to the level of my terrible judgment, heavy cream, sugar, eggs, salt. Katrina dropped in the basil and I mixed that in too. Catherine was lazy in her watching; she had, after all, rolled out the pie crust herself. I kept asking her if the rolling pin hurt her hands. Your wrists, I said. Doesn't the pressure burn? I had no idea making a crust was so repetitious. She said pain wasn't so bad when she could predict it. You understand, she said, giving me a wink. I said she was right and when they went to the basement to check noises they thought were coming from the furnace—old houses, and all that, or so they said—I turned my phone back on and listened to three voicemails. I sprinkled dried elderberries on top of the pie as it cooled. I was alone.

The first voicemail, like the second, and the third, informed me that my father had a life-threatening medical emergency. Each call came from a woman who identified herself as a prison chaplain. I kept thinking, This means he's dead. But he wasn't, not yet, though he had tried to be. The chaplain did not use my first name but my last, and used the prefix Mx. instead of Miss. Instead of wondering about my father, I thought, Is she a feminist? Is she very young or very old or neither? I wondered if she was a lesbian. I wondered if human resource meetings covered gender-neutral pronouns. When the pie was done, I told them I loved to be sick and they said that made them happy. They couldn't have known the pie was no longer for me.

Before night broke the day, Catherine ushered us out of the temporary home and into the car. I lay down in the back seat without my seatbelt on. She helped me position two scarves to form a pillow. I asked the wives to check the trunk to make sure my mother hadn't slipped in. Katrina told me to close my eyes and I did. Me in the back, child again. For years we did not have a car, and I envied those around me. Legs not swollen from pavement walking. Knees not stiff from ocean chill. Being taken by the wives exceeded all expectations of good. Even of great. Between my thighs, the pie sat safe and still. In my pocket, a small bottle of elderberry syrup, made under Catherine's watch. She said that I was being a good girl and that I would be rewarded with good pie once we arrived at a newly favorite park of theirs for our picnic. I released a shriek.

Shoot, she said. What is it? I heard her turn the car off.

I told the wives I was actually terrible. I tasted snot in my mouth and realized I had begun to weep. To the wives, I added, It's the jail.

Katrina said, Your mom's back in already? Her expression revealed she was not surprised.

I said, No. I said, My dad's sick. I wondered if my mother

knew and if my aunt had been able to borrow a car so they could visit. I pressed my knuckles into the curves of my stomach. I thought, Dying, dying, dying, dead. I emitted a growl, believing it to be a cry, and when the wives jumped in their seats, I did too. I wanted to tell them to go away, to leave me be, but I was too tired to fight attention. Instead, I asked Catherine what she would do.

What I would do, she said. If it were my father, you mean? Or if it were yours? I asked her what the difference would be and she said her father was a good man. Anyway, she said. Did they transfer him to a real hospital?

I said, Yeah. I repeated the coded language the chaplain used in her voicemails: attempt, investigate, clarify. I told the wives I'd never known my father to have suicidal ideation but I'd also never known him to not be depressed. His depression, like mine, thrived not in sadness but in irritation. Mouths carrying stink and yellow. Clothes worn down to holes in the thighs. Snapping at everyone who moved. I fantasized about my father in a vulnerable state, offering him comfort and he accepting it. I imagined what life might have been like had my father been the sort of depressed person that is most loved by others: quiet, tearful, low-energy but functional, responsible for themselves, not a risk, but too tender to be held accountable for minor social failures. I did not know how to offer comfort to a person so like myself.

Catherine told me I should sleep, that I still looked terrible. I asked her to be me. She said, What?

I said, Catherine. Come on. I repeated what my father had done, or what he had tried to do, and the wives looked at each other, uncomfortable. No one likes hearing those words, after all. I said, Please.

She said, I don't know what you mean. I told her I needed her to call and get more information. You know my name, I said. You know me. Beside her, Katrina shrugged. I added that her wife could not do it because, like me, she was driven by an innate sense of guilt. Again, her wife shrugged, as if to say, Well, she is correct! To that Catherine said, Jesus Christ.

Catherine took my phone while Katrina held my hands from the front seat. She told me I was being wonderfully calm. I know this is a cliche, she said, but it's not your fault.

I said, Are you serious? It is obviously my fault. I rubbed her hands in mine, as I realized the skin was cold cold cold. I sensed I was again becoming hot hot hot. Katrina told me she was being serious and she was proud of me for keeping it together. She described me as a bit of a flight risk in an emergency.

I said, Flight risk? I let out a deep scream and both women jumped in their seats. Catherine glared at me and told me I'd made her hang up.

I'm going to have to call again, she said. Please scream inside of yourself for a few minutes, okay?

It was a reasonable request. I took Katrina's hands in mine once more and watched Catherine prepare to embody me. I wondered if she would go the unstable, hysterical daughter route. Would she work up a few tears? Would she yell about the system? Maybe she would bring up a lawsuit. She seemed to come from that sort of family, the type of people who know how to make vague legal threats with confidence.

When Catherine spoke, the words melded into my brain and dissipated. I couldn't have repeated them back even then. I was transfixed by the way her face contorted, a level of acting I had not anticipated. Her eyes took on a hurt look, that of a weak bandage, and her pitch dropped into a wound. I thought, Do I possibly seem so aching? Am I so visibly shaken by every disruption. Do I project such a small degree of peace. When she was done, I asked not about the details of my father's situation, but about what possessed her.

She said, You. She looked at me with what I guessed was love or something like it. Katrina added that they paid attention. She told me I was being a good girl, the best girl, that she could not be happier or prouder of the way I was behaving. I felt warm dribble against my insides. I was thinking of my mother washing her hands with bars of white soap, not knowing. Or worse: knowing and scrubbing cuticles till they revealed pink meat underneath.

Catherine asked if I was finally satisfied. I was, though I was too heightened to see it then. I told her to get out of the driver's seat. She said, What?

I said, Please. I felt entirely prepared to smash her nose against the steering wheel if she needed convincing.

She said, You want to drive? I should drive.

I unbuckled my seatbelt and put my hands on her sternum. She stiffened and stared not at Katrina but straight ahead. Her body felt small and active beneath my fingers. I said, Catherine. I told her she understood.

We three were quiet on the drive to the hospital. Not far from the jail, and also not far from the border of Vermont, we sustained a comfortable refusal to look at one another. No road games, no fingers in my mouth, no driving barefoot. Katrina spent most of the drive on her phone and Catherine stared through the windshield. I asked if she was willing cars to spin into us and she only put both hands to my neck and asked me to please be quiet. I felt so grateful for her touch, to be seen, to be reminded that I was flesh existing in a space and not only a figment, not only an emotion. I said, Sure. I said, Okay.

In the parking lot, the wives talked through our infinite possibilities. The warden might say no. They might say yes. They might not be available at all. There's probably a social worker available, Catherine offered. There has to be some kind of backup. Katrina agreed: the chain of command couldn't hinge on just one person. I did not correct them because my eyes hurt. I focused only on what I felt was becoming clearer and crisper to me as I continued thinking about my dead brother and my dying grandmother and my death-driven father. If my mother and I were the only ones left, I wondered, would she finally care for me or would I be as alone as ever.

I asked the wives for hairpins. I said, My scalp feels greasy. Katrina handed me a few from her purse and told me I looked holy. I knew she loved me when she did not point out that my hair looked cleaner than usual, given that she'd shampooed it herself. I promised I'd see them soon.

I put the pie to my chest. I heard them say, Okay, with a lot of concern but neither put their hands on me or tried to stop me, and so I found my way across the parking lot (mostly full, mostly gray), through the front doors (glass, sliding, littered with fingerprints), by the front desk (I was called back a step or two, I'll admit, to sign my name on a piece of white lined paper and receive a name tag), up the elevator (empty, including myself), and to my father's floor without qualm. Each step leading me to my father, I only thought, I am good I am smart I am figuring this out I am a good daughter I am excellent I am not at fault here. I continued this train of self-reassurance even when I saw two uniformed police officers standing near my father's door, talking and fiddling on a desktop computer. From over their shoulders, I watched them scroll the pages of a used muscle car website before they walked in the other direction. I thought, Perfect.

31

THE DOOR TO MY FATHER'S ROOM WAS closed. I wondered if my mother was inside already, if her sister had indeed been able to borrow a car. I wanted her there to lessen the pressure on me and yet I felt my childhood envy too, imagining my parents only needing each other and ignoring me. She still hadn't reached out since being released. I fingered the knob, expecting to be shouted at for my presence, but when I entered the world did not change. I thought, I did it! I felt accomplished, finished, completed. At his bedside, I leaned down, and he opened his eyes. I said, Dad? He told me to fuck myself.

I said, What? I felt weak, dizzy. I put my hands on my hips to steady my core and perhaps look intimidating. I puffed my chest out, like I'd seen thin, bright women do while bickering in public with their boyfriends.

My father only blinked, his eyes enormous purple sores. I said, Did somebody hit you? He said he didn't remember shit. I asked if he was feeling okay, if the black eyes came before or after the thing that happened, and he said he couldn't remember. He said life was shit but he was glad to be out of that rat cage. I told him I understood. I told him I was glad he was still here. I asked if he had it in his head to get out of jail for a week, a check-in with the rest of the world. I guessed he understood what I was getting at, the sick question I wasn't quite asking, because he only looked at me; I thought he saw all I had inherited from her. I wondered what it might be like to reach my father's age and still not feel seen, feel witnessed, and decided I could not tempt fate, could not seal my own future as karma for inaction. I repeated that I was glad he was still there and he blinked a couple times, face dry, and wiggled his wrists.

He said, Girl, hey. He told me not to get all hysterical on him in a place like this. He said, Uncuff me, would you? He nodded to my head.

I said, Sure. I was guilty enough to help him have a taste of what he'd wanted all along: freedom. I pulled the bobby pins from my hair and made okay work of it. Not as fast as I'd been as a kid, when my father taught me, but quick enough. When I was done, he shook his wrists out and put his hands around my throat.

I said, Dad. He was not squeezing. Only holding. I found him tender.

He said, Helen. He said, This is your fault.

I said, It's the system's fault. He told me not to be a smartass. He kept his hands loose but steady and we spent time looking at each other. My father and I share many of the same features: noses bent to the right, gapped teeth at the bottom, hair that grows flat and without a shape. I asked if he thought Ryan would look like me if he were alive and without hesitation, he said, Not a chance. He told me Ryan was a very pretty child and I agreed. A nurse aide knocked at the door and my father moved his hands to my shoulders and tugged me down into a hug. He smelled like white soap.

Shit, the aide said. Did you do that? You can't just uncuff people.

Oh, I said, still bent over my father. Sorry.

He said, You have to stand up now. Someone has to fix this. I thought the aide looked silly, so annoyed, in his yellow scrubs. The room's one window let in little light and he appeared to me as muted, subdued. I wondered if this lack of brightness allowed workers to be more honest. Not feeling pressure to smile is a universal relief.

I said, Fix it? I said, I can fix it. I motioned to recuff my father and he nodded like an angel. I closed the cuffs. I imagined flipping my father's bed. For what? To cause a ruckus, to get attention for myself. To listen to my father's head hit the linoleum. To make his breath catch. To give him a slightly improved chance of escape. The aide told me not to be irresponsible. He said if I ever saw someone like that, uncuffed and wild, I had to report it to him.

I said, To you, specifically? He looked me eyebrows to ankles and said yes. I almost pointed out the guards outside the door but didn't want him to call them in. From his bed, my father cleared his throat.

When the aide left, my father said, Helen, come on. He said, You can make it right.

I said, I came because I was worried about you. I told him what the messages said, what the system would have on record for him. I did not ask him if the reports were accurate or why he did what he did. He nodded and let his eyes sit neutral while I spoke. Down the hall, a man screamed noise, no words.

He said, You didn't sign in, did you? I lied and said no. He said, People would believe you were scared, right? I'm practically a convict. I didn't correct him and said, Yeah. He said, You can do it again. You can do it and we'll be happier. He promised me he would wait to leave the room until long after I'd be gone. He'd sit in his bed like a boy, he said. Watching the wall stay the same. Feeling urine build in his bladder. He'd sit and jiggle his feet while I was in the elevator and out the door. He told me everything would be fine.

I said, Does Mom know you're here? My mind always went to logistics when on the brink of making a bad decision. Where is everyone, what time is it, where were we just before and where will we be after. One, two, three. There is stability in what can be named.

He said, Yeah.

I said, Does she know why? I worried my mother would blame herself. I wondered if she'd try to visit the hospital immediately or wait for permission from the warden. Her stakes were higher than mine, as her movements were more monitored. I felt alive with the spans of what I could get away with. I felt, fleetingly, that it was time to do something for my family, to test just how alike we really were. I thought of these things to not think of my father or mother as sad beings.

He looked away. He said, If you know, I guess she does. He told me he didn't tell anybody shit. These people could give a man some discretion, you know.

I know, I said. The world doesn't need to know our shit. I said, I won't tell Grandma. I felt like a good girl then, keeping quiet about hours alone with a sick small boy.

Thanks, he said. Yeah, tell her it's some bullshit UTI, whatever. Still looking away from me in shame I understood he was so much a slice of me we could not be evaluated separately. He asked me about the cuffs again, faux confidence regained. I asked him what the good was going to be.

He said, What?

On the phone, I said. You were convinced life was going to get better once you got out. He nodded and I realized he was actually listening to me. I felt shy in this new dynamic, but pushed myself to continue. I want you to tell me what you imagine happening, I said.

Shit, he said. See your mom. Go to some meetings. Hit up Cumbie's. He laughed and I smiled but did not pull noise out of myself. He told me I was gonna make him cry, turn him into a real pussy, and still I stayed smiling, not laughing, and down the hall, people hollered at one another to eat shit and to settle down.

I'd pick up your mom, he said, and I nodded, though we both knew he didn't have a valid license nor a car. Go up to the graveyard with some smokes and have dinner. Catch the sunset, you remember? Turns the water pink.

My brother's grave rested midway up a hill overlooking the bay in our hometown. Tourists driving up always thought that spot looked real nice, perfect for photos or a picnic, this mound of green with a view of half the town. On clear days, Boston waited in the distance. Only lifers like my parents brought dollar slices and candy up there. I never sat at Ryan's grave, never ate with him or talked to him. I turned into myself, went still, numbed out. I hadn't been in years and going back was not something I wanted, not a closure I fantasized about.

I told him to eat some of the pie. He said, What? I repeated myself and reminded him he loved pie. I projected emotions I was not sure I had ever recognized in him before: joy, relief, peace. This evening was not the first time I realized my father's core concept of family did not extend to me, but it was the first time I understood this distance as a permission to find my own. I decided my father and I were giving each other gifts.

I said, Berries are fresh.

He said, Not from a can? His eyebrows went up and I imagined sleeping in his forehead wrinkles.

I confirmed: not from a can. I put the pie on his bed and told him I wanted to see him eat it. Not all of it, I said. I don't want you to puke. He told me he never minded puke and I said, Well, fine. Puke. I lied and told him I made the pie just for him, because I remembered how much he loved the ones at the jail and when I was a kid.

He said, Uncuff me. I imagined my mother entering and decided I would not cuff them together but knock myself out, forehead to wall, and let them leave me behind without the slow awkwardness of goodbye.

I was thinking of yesterday's fever, the clarity I was embracing after being entirely vulnerable and spent. I told him he'd understand once he ate and he gave me a look and I went on, I couldn't stop myself, I told him we were the same and we would get the same good, and he told me he wasn't hungry, and that's when I said, Eat the fucking pie.

Understand I had never felt so powerful or so worthy of almost love. I was giving my father the gift I wanted, the one that even the wives had not yet entirely delivered. My mother would nurse my father, I told myself, though I knew it was more likely an actual nurse would find him here in the hospital. A coded alert might go around, reminders to kitchen staff to make sure they weren't undercooking the meat—And could the maintenance staff make sure no bottles were leaking chemicals onto the bed trays? I trusted my father would understand what I'd given him then, what I'd gone and done to show how much and in what way we were the same.

My father ducked his head to his wrist still cuffed to the bedpost and worked his fingers into the pie. He said, What is this? I told him elderberry. He said, Filling's a little undercooked, no?

I said, It's supposed to be like that. I watched him eat, knuckles to mouth, and told myself I was good. I was a good daughter, a good person. For a brief time, a good sister. I had never put the bobby pin back into my hair so I had one less step when I moved to uncuff my father. One less opportunity to think about what was right in front of me. A man who, like myself, wanted every inaccessible joy.

When the filling was mostly gone, I dropped the plastic pie dish into the trash. He wiggled his fingers and I cleaned him with wet wipes from the dresser, thinking of my grandmother and her doll. I asked if he wanted the TV on and he said, Nah. He said he had a lot of thinking to do. I didn't ask him what about and I believe he was grateful for that. We did not embrace but we did give each other a nod. Beyond him, I checked for my mother's profile in the window but was met with only wind.

As I left his room, one of the officers previously at the computer stopped me. He said, Hey, lady. Above us, fluorescents.

I imagined breaking into a run. I imagined tattling on my father. Instead, I said, What?

He said, You a visitor? You're supposed to have your name tag on. He looked like the kind of man who would call me a dyke on the sidewalk.

I pulled the crumpled tag from my pocket and told him I was going to be sick. He put his hands up as though I'd screamed and told me to find a bathroom down the hall.

The bathroom was as promised: down the hall, single-stall, empty. I thought vaguely of Emma and worried for her. As I vomited, I imagined the myriad ways my father would almost certainly get caught. Did he want to escape, really? I thought no. I thought my father was a man who would want to take a walk around the hospital and put himself back to bed. A man who would order a coffee and drink it in the courtyard. A man who might shit himself from my poorly prepared pie and know I'd done it on purpose. We're made of the same stuff, after all. In the mirror, I reminded myself I could not die, not yet, not without seeing the face that could never come find me.

32

WHEN I FOUND THE WIVES, THEY WERE not in the car. I'd checked and found it empty, prompting my panic that they had abandoned me. I wondered if my father had made his way to the parking lot and killed them. I imagined him en route to the woods with their bodies over his shoulders. So eager was I to confess to the nearest person about my role in their deaths that I mumbled it to myself, over and over. A sliver of reality pressed me to walk through hospital property before confessing and it was down a long corridor where I saw the wives speaking to each other.

As I approached, I imagined them arguing, serious in spite of, or perhaps because of, the pile of Little Debbies in Catherine's arms. They were probably only reminiscing about a gluten-free and vegan version of the chocolate cakes they were holding but I liked to pull anxiety in from all corners when I could manage it. I wondered if this was enough chaos to splinter them. Which one would stomp off and which would shuffle me into their car, hurrying me so I did not catch pneumonia. Which one would call over and over and over and leave voicemails and long long text messages. Which would love me more. I surprised myself by realizing I did not want them to shatter but to stay solid. I did not want chaos but calm. I neared them and they did not appear to sense me, did not even glance toward me, and some of our magic was lost. I understood them as only women, only ordinary, only like myself, though better.

She needs time, Katrina said. I can't even imagine what I would do if one of my parents tried to . . .

I know, Catherine said. I know. But isn't this, like, traumatic? She can't just run around this place trying to find him.

So, we do what? Tempt her back with photos of a dozen cakes?

Maybe not, Catherine said. We can find a closet and take some pictures with your shirt off. Katrina told her wife she was feeling puffy and that maybe Catherine should try it instead. Then she put her face in her hands and I realized she was trying not to laugh. The situation was surreal, bizarre, and with my secret, only more so. I knew then I could not tell them I'd uncuffed my father and left him. That I had been reckless, stupid, foolish. That I would still do most anything to be chosen by people who did not particularly care for me. My entire life could crumble if my father ratted me out. I put one hand on each of their wrists, causing them both to jump, and told them we had to find a closet.

The wives said, What?

I explained we needed a closet, any closet. I need to be in the dark, I said. I need to know something for sure. The wives followed me out of the cafeteria and down several long hallways. At each set of automatic doors, I panicked, believing we needed an ID to proceed, and each time, I was incorrect. We only needed to press a button and wait.

Katrina held my hand while Catherine opened various closet doors, each just a slit. She told me no, no, no, so many times no that I wondered if she was going to reject every option in some effort to counter my bizarre behaviors. Close to the exit, she opened a door all the way and told me to hurry up.

Stand right in front of it, I said. Press your backs to it. They nodded. When I closed myself in what appeared to be a janitorial closet, I waited until I felt a certain pressure, rested against some plywood, and placed the knuckles of both my hands into my mouth. My jaw resisted and I waited for my eyes to prickle. Tears came slower than I hoped but I pressed my teeth into my skin and sped up the release. I was as alone as I could stand to be, with my perpetual rage and sadness, and could not quiet my mind enough to count the seconds. I had given my father two gifts: a chance at autonomy, and, more important to me, a chance to be sick. When I made that pie, I wanted to be sick again and again. I wanted to begin my new life being cared for with hot water and washcloths and thermometers. And I gave my father slice after slice after slice of that hope. I imagined my mother sleeping beneath my father's mattress, rolling out when aides exited so she could care for him, the only being she felt was family. Gifts, gifts. I was resolved, then; I had made my right decision and it was the one that scared me.

I knocked on the door and the wives stepped away so I

could exit. I need to drive again, I said as we left the hospital. I felt there was one person I had to warn. I promised the wives life was getting better, not worse. They said, Uh huh. During the drive, they fed me with their fingers and I felt an incredible power. They'd seen my instability and still offered me every bit of control and for that my love congealed. As I drove, I wondered if my father had yet run or walked or struggled to the toilet.

As we digested, the wives must have sensed my anxiety, my thoughts rotating between dad dad dad dad and stupid stupid stupid stupid stupid, as Catherine told Katrina to turn on the radio. Music can be soothing, she said. I told them not to, as I was terrified about what the news might tell us. Had my father tried to escape and been caught already? Was anyone looking for me? Checking cameras from the parking lot, looking for license plate numbers. A report would still be opaque at that time, I assumed, only telling of a lockdown at the hospital, noting that one floor contained inmates from several local corrections facilities. But I would know.

Even just commercials, Katrina said. The local ones can be fun.

I said, Fun? I thought pulling my esophagus from my ears sounded fun. Katrina ignored my tone and fiddled with the dial until we landed on a local station. See, she said. They're advertising a mattress place.

Good support, Catherine said. You know, for your emotions.

As I drove I kept my hands on the wheel. My body was not my body but a stiffness. My worries increased: What if there was already national news? Did these stations pick up breaking alerts across state borders? As we got closer to the person I needed to see, we got farther from my father. I tried to imagine him eating a vanilla pudding cup but could only see him smiling up at the ceiling, waiting and waiting. I regretted not asking him if he enjoyed not having a bunk bed for a few nights. In the hours it took to reach the nursing home, we heard only forgettable pop and advertisements for moving companies, juice cleanses, and private daycares. One at-home elder care advertisement came on and Katrina said, Doesn't that sound like a prison to you? And when I gave her a look, she looked to Catherine sheepishly, who only said, Jesus.

We signed into the nursing home under our real names. I led the women to my grandmother's room, embarrassed at the building's plainness. The facility was perfectly adequate: clean, calm, quiet. Sterile, I imagined, as much as a state-funded place could be. I never caught the staff yelling or pushing or abandoning. The food was always cooked properly. But I could not ignore the quickness of Catherine's eyes, the sadness in them, the pity. In the hallway outside her room, I hesitated, and the wives mimicked me. I told them they really didn't have to do this. I won't be upset if you head to the car, I said. I'll understand if you need to take off.

Will you be sad? Katrina asked. If we leave? I paused, unsure, and then said I might be.

But I would understand, I said. It's fine. This is a lot. Two women wheeled a woman down the hallway, quiet and, I guessed, content. I said, I would understand, but I would be unhappy. I said, I wouldn't be fine at all. I said, I'm only close to being functional because of you.

Katrina said, Do you think about what your life would be like if you listened to us? She told me to think about it. You shouldn't trust yourself so much, she said. You make horrible decisions.

I was about to repeat my refrain: I was horrible, I did not deserve them. I nearly confessed to my latest mistake, but then Catherine put her palms to our mouths and gestured for me to enter first. Come on, she said to me. I froze, imagining my mother feeding my grandmother yellow noodles. The wives took my hands and I led them inside the room.

My grandmother was up and dancing her doll in her lap. She was in a good mood that day. A yes mood. I wondered if she would mention our sleepover. I said, Hello, beautiful! She said the same to me. She turned the doll toward us. When Catherine and Katrina complimented the doll, her pretty face and her darling outfit, I wanted to kiss them both. Love, I thought. Yes, there it is.

I hope you don't mind visitors, I said. I know it isn't my usual day, but my friends really wanted to meet you.

She patted the bed beside her. There was not enough room for any adult to fit. She did not yet have a new roommate, and she also did not have extra furniture. Both armchairs had been removed. We three stood beside her in a row, me closest, then Katrina, then Catherine.

Tell me about yourselves, she said. I want to know who is around my good girl. The wives introduced themselves, sparing the obvious details. When Katrina said she used to be a ballerina, my grandmother asked her to show her something, a twirl, she requested, and Katrina, to my surprise, managed a series of four or five pirouettes in her sneakers. My grand-mother clapped and whooped, to which Katrina said it wasn't her best work, but she was glad she had one fan. When Catherine said she taught literature, my grandmother commented that it sounded very fancy. She doesn't teach English, my grandmother said to Katrina and me in a stage whisper, but literature! Even Catherine laughed.

Look, my grandmother said. I wondered if she was seeing my father over my shoulder. Lurking in the window. Dangling from the ceiling. I told myself he was still in bed, pretending to be cuffed, a good boy, waiting to take an easy walk around the building. To eat an ice cream in the courtyard. To flirt with a cashier in the cafeteria. I told myself I understood him, we two beasts in want of small pleasures.

To my grandmother, I said, Where? I did look around then, at her bureau and on her side table, wondering if perhaps my mother really had been by. Had she left a note? A letter? A gift? But nothing looked amiss. Her wet wipes, red-and-white candies, pine air freshener. One bottle of mauve nail polish. Two hairbrushes and a comb. Every other visit, I had cleaned out my grandmother's hair with my fingers. A gift. I said, Gram, where?

She ignored me.

I checked her bathroom: all normal. I got on my knees and checked under her bed: also all normal. I walked to the empty side of the room and pulled the divider curtain all the way shut, then all the way open. I said, Grams, am I really looking for something? Or are you teasing me? I suspected this was all a game, a ruse, but I could not let the notion rest. What couldn't I see, what was just out of sight. Had my grandmother herself written something—a memory, a confession, an honesty she could not bear to speak? But nothing was unusual. Well, that was not true. The laughter, the goodness, the full room. That was unusual, but I believed then that change was not deserving of my focus.

I stood at the window and took in my wives and my grandmother. I said, Gram, did I find it yet? Did you see me crawling all over your floor?

Look, she said, grinning, mostly toothless. Look, look, look.

I frowned with my smile. I said, Gram, I am looking! Can I have a hint? I thought I was going to drop and crack myself open. I thought I was hearing stars at noon.

She shook her head at me. You don't need a hint, she said. You see it. It's right here!

I said, Where? I looked to the wives and they only shrugged, amused and baffled too. I said, Gram, I think you won this game. I don't see a thing out of place.

She said, Helen!

I said, Gram! You called me Helen. I said, That's my name! A momentary bliss, a distraction. I told myself, Dad will pretend to be asleep and let the aide fix the cuffs, believing it was a mistake. Dad will fall and pretend it was a fluke. Dad will piss and shit his bed and no one will notice much in the agitated rush to wipe him. I told myself, He will only call my mother and fill a silence. He will only sit in dignity and commit it to memory.

My grandmother looked at me like I was ridiculous. Of

course I know your name, she said. Now, Helen, open that blind. All the way up. I did as she instructed. The lift cord was not the best, so it took a few tries, but I worked the blind all the way to the top. A great white shuttled in. The aides did not keep the blinds open like this, perhaps trying not to disrupt people's naps with the light. I had never seen the room quite so warm. She said, There it is!

I turned from the window. My wives and my grandmother, illuminated. All three shielding their eyes with their hands, faces on me, laughing, laughing. I said, Oh! I saw it. I still see it—most of the time.

Acknowledgments

Thank you to my editor, Alicia Kroell, for seeing the potential in this strange book and finding a home for it with Catapult. Thank you to the entire team, including but not limited to Lena Moses-Schmitt, Miriam Vance, Laura Berry, Elizabeth Pankova, Wah-Ming Chang, Rachel Fershleiser, and Megan Fishmann, for your dedication. Thank you to Katie Grimm for making me a better writer, to Caroline Miranda and Monique Vieu for thoughtful and vigorous feedback, and to everyone at Don Congdon for their support. Thank you to escitalopram (10 mg) for helping me live. To my dearest friends: You know who you are, and thank you. To my wife: Being loved by you is the great honor of my life. Thank you. To my dead: Your hands are here. To my young self: Thank you for surviving.

MARISSA HIGGINS (she/her/hers) is a lesbian writer. *A Good Happy Girl* is her first novel.